MW00905813

Surviving Rapture

KAI KIRIYAMA

xoxo

Kai Kiriy

ISBN: 1532730373
ISBN-13: 978-15132730375

To the Dreamers.
To the Rebels.
To the Builders, who act upon their dreams.

CHAPTER ONE

The Rapture

The apocalypse happened, and humanity capitalized on it. When the dead rose from their graves and began devouring the flesh of the living, humanity somehow found a way to turn a profit. Big game hunting was no longer a thing that obnoxiously rich people did for sport. They had no need to hunt lions when safaris full of zombies cropped up, seemingly overnight. The hordes were corralled, those that weren't destroyed immediately were left in cities that were beyond saving, and perimeters were set up to keep them in. Theme parks filled with the shambling undead were attractions in Japan and parts of Russia, where you could pay for the luxury of roughing it in a monitored but deserted city, just like in the movies.

Despite it all, nobody capitalized on the apocalypse better than the Americans. In true American fashion, they turned the apocalypse into a game show.

Everyone was automatically entered in the lottery. Contestants were chosen randomly once a year to participate in the brutal reality program. Entire cities were evacuated and walled off, monitored by military officers in full riot gear and armed to the teeth while the "winners" of the lottery were drugged and dragged away in the middle of the night.

They called it "The Rapture" and it was the highest grossing television event in the history of television events. Corporate sponsors ranged from Coca-Cola to Nike shoes. The Rapture was a bigger success than the Olympics and the Oscars combined. Everyone wanted in on the action. The "winners" of the events were given huge paychecks and were made into overnight celebrities.

Aya groaned and forced herself to roll over. She had been set on her side as she slept off the drugs. She ran a hand over her face, resting her forearm over her eyes. She didn't remember getting grabbed She'd been on her way home from the grocery store, dragging a little cart full of fresh produce behind her. She hadn't been wearing headphones; she had to be too careful to allow herself to be distracted by that. She lifted her arm to look at her wrist as she noticed a heavy, silver cuff clamped onto her wrist.

"Motherfuckers," Aya muttered to herself. She forced herself to sit up, despite the spinning of the world that threatened to make her throw up. She didn't need any other explanation. She knew she'd been picked for The Rapture.

She peered around the dim room she'd been dropped in. Everything was dusty and warm. There was a sick feeling in Aya's guts and she tried to shake it off, a pulling at a memory buried in the back of her mind. She spied her bag on the floor by the doorway and she forced herself to crawl across the room to fetch it - she knew there was no way she'd be able to walk without stumbling all over the place like a drunk for at least an hour. She just hoped that this wasn't a ploy to kill her off quickly. Aya wasn't exactly the biggest fan of The Rapture, and she wasn't surprised that she'd finally been picked. She had been a thorn in the proverbial foot of the government-sanctioned killing spree that constituted the gameplay of The Rapture since she was sixteen. Her parents had been protesting since she was fourteen and the Rapture had been originally introduced. Now, she was twenty-two, sitting in a musty old house with a metal bracelet that would monitor her vitals and had a countdown timer for her to keep track of how much time was left in the three-day event she found herself trapped in, fumbling through her bag for her phone and the bottle of water she knew would still be there.

Aya cracked the cap on her water and gulped it greedily, downing half the bottle without thinking about rations. She leaned against the wall and waited for the room to stop spinning before turning her attentions to the bracelet she was forced to wear. The timer was still green, and still had three and a half hours left on it. That meant she had three and a half hours until the game started. Three and a half hours to figure out what the hell she was going to do.

She looked at her phone. At least they'd been kind enough not to smash it into a million pieces. They were affording her one phone call, which was a courtesy she'd not expected. She dialled, waiting for the line to pick up.

"Aya?"

"Hey, mom," she replied, her voice cracking. "You sound like you've been crying."

"You've been gone for ten hours."

"I was drugged."

"I know. Are you hurt?"

"Just working the drugs out of my system."

There was an audible sigh and Aya smiled. Her mother was muttering curses in Mandarin under her breath. She'd inherited her mother's looks and proclivity for profanity, but she'd inherited her father's stubbornness, and rest his soul, his patience. Aya looked around the room, taking in the old hardwood floor, covered in a gaudy area rug, the olive green walls, the big window and the new door that seemed very out of place to be set in a living room. Her eyes rested on the antique wood-burning stove before taking in the new furniture. There was a beep from the heart rate monitor on her wrist and she didn't care. She knew the place where she'd been dropped. Not much had changed, except for the furniture. Memories flooded back into Aya's mind and she felt tears threatening to overwhelm her. She swallowed back her emotion, refusing to allow either the Controllers, or her mother, know that she was ready to cry. She wouldn't give the Controllers the satisfaction of knowing that they'd succeeded in catching her that far off her guard - they'd already managed to kidnap her and force her into the Program, she wouldn't give them any more satisfaction. Her mother, on the other hand, was still sniffling into the phone and Aya knew that she needed to be stronger than she was feeling, or at least pretend to be stronger than she was feeling, if only for her mother's sake.

"Mom?" she whispered. "You're not going to believe this, but I'm back on the farm."

"Son of a whore!"

Aya chuckled. "It's okay. At least I know where I am."

"They're doing it to break you."

"I won't let it. Don't worry. I'll see you in three days."

"Be careful. I love you."

"I love you, too. I'll make you proud."

"You already have."

Aya felt her heart catch in her throat. She wanted to cry, to beg her mom to come and help her. She knew where she was, and it wouldn't be hard for her mom to find her. She knew she could stay put until a helicopter could be dispatched. She wasn't too proud to beg and her mom wouldn't hesitate to use her significant influence to get her only daughter out of The Rapture. She also knew that any unauthorized aircraft would be shot down immediately. Aya held her tongue, choking back her feelings, forcing the words back down, swallowing hard and not letting her desperate desires overcome her. She took a deep breath and said the only words that seemed appropriate given the circumstances.

"Bye, mom."

"Goodbye, Aya."

Aya hung up her phone and forced herself to get up. The world spun angrily, her head pounding and her stomach roiling. She stumbled across the room and leaned heavily against the wall. Closing her eyes, she willed the spinning to stop, begging the dizziness to go away. She'd heard rumours about what the drugs they used to sedate the contestants were, everything from chloroform to diazepam and everything in between. No one knew for sure and Aya wasn't sure if her symptoms were normal or not. Her body felt heavy and sluggish, like she was coming down with a cold, and the dizziness didn't help.

"Okay," Aya muttered to herself. "This is beyond stupid. You're not gonna throw up, Aya. And even if you do, so what? They'll just broadcast it and slander you more than they already are. Big deal. If you puke on national television, maybe you'll get some sympathy."

She chuckled to herself, a bitter and mirthless sound.

"Fabulous," she decided with a shake of her head. She winced as the motion made her world start to tilt and spin again. Aya sighed. "You've gotta work through this, you don't have time to waste," she told herself.

She cast a glance up at the obvious cameras on the walls and sneered. She didn't know if they were live already or not, and she didn't care to know. With another sigh, she pushed herself away from the wall, keeping her hand flat to steady herself against the dizziness as she took a tentative step forward.

There was a lot of work that needed to be done if she expected to outlast The Rapture.

CHAPTER TWO

Aya

Aya was twelve when the apocalypse had happened. She had been dragged out of her farmhouse, the only place she had ever known, late at night by her frantic parents as the world fell apart around her. They stole away in the night and climbed into their SUV, Aya curled up, sobbing in the backseat and holding tightly to her border collie. Her father, Arthur Hammond, was a doctor, her mother, Lila Wu, was a sociology professor and a known activist for human rights across the globe.

The roads leading to town were deserted; there were no signs of life on the highway anywhere. Her parents spoke quietly, voices urgent and clipped. They were making plans to get away. They had always thought they had been safe in the middle of nowhere. There were so few neighbours that there was no way a pandemic would reach them.

Unfortunately, the zombie rising hadn't been particularly picky about who got sick. Once it had developed into a strain of pathogen that no longer needed to latch on to a weak or sickly host, there was very little to stop it from attacking the healthier people who believed their immune systems and vaccinations would protect them.

Aya hadn't stopped screaming when she saw the first zombies shambling down the dirt road toward their idyllic farmhouse until her father showed up with his gun. Her father had ordered his family back into the house, to pack quickly. Aya had cowered, covering her ears with tears streaming down her face as her dog stood guard, growling incessantly. The shotgun firing rang through the house and Aya screamed again. Her dog crossed the room and licked her elbow once, calming her.

Aya's mother returned, frantic as she dragged suitcases full of clothes and irreplaceable items behind her. It didn't take long for her to help Aya pack.

No one was stopped on the road; there were no vehicles and no one hitchhiking. They drove in tense silence, Arthur glaring out the windshield and Lila staring out her window, keeping an eye out for any signs of life. The people in the surrounding farms were not necessarily friends with the Wu family, but they had known one another from various farming deals and meeting at the local community centre.

"Do you think...?" Lila asked before trailing off.

"I'm trying not to," Arthur replied.

Aya buried her face in her dog's neck and tried not to cry anymore. It wasn't a long trip to make it to town, half an hour. They passed through the small hamlet that the highway passed through, there was no other way to get around it, and they tried not to linger for long.

Fires still burned and the air was thick with smoke. Windows had been broken in the convenience store on the corner, and bodies littered the lawns of the few houses that lined the main street. Whether they were human casualties or zombies, it was hard to say. Arthur didn't stop the car as they passed the church. The windows were brightly lit, but there was no sound coming from within. It was more than likely that everyone inside was praying that they'd stay safe.

Aya stared, wide-eyed as they passed, seeing a shadow move across the window and she hoped that no one inside had been hurt.

Arthur pressed the gas pedal, speeding up as they drove up the incline, following the highway away from the hamlet, ignoring the horrors that they knew were hidden out of sight of the main road. Everything was too empty, too quiet, and no one dared to speak their fears, in case the dead would hear them and force them to fight their way out. It didn't take long for the road to become cluttered as they moved away from the hamlet. The closer they got to the other town, the more abandoned cars they found dotting the highway. Some were overturned in the ditch. Others were just parked, empty, as the occupants had made a break for it. The highway lights were few and far between, and Arthur was thankful for it - he didn't need his wife and daughter seeing clearly the horrors that surrounded the highway and the cars parked and abandoned there. Eventually, Arthur was forced to slow their progress as the road became filled with people, survivors of the zombie rising all clamouring to get past the highway and into the safety of the town.

The roads were barricaded off as the military had moved in, setting up their base in the town closest to the river. It was the largest of the local towns, it had the most amenities and the largest population It was logical that the hospital would be filled with people falling ill and the military wanted to reduce as many casualties as possible. The survivors from the surrounding areas had been stopped by a hastily erected fence and a line of military vehicles.

Everyone was angry, and Aya could hear the various shouts through the windows of their SUV. The military officers in charge of the barricade weren't letting people through and no one was getting any straight answers.

Arthur parked the car and told Aya and Lila to stay put.

It didn't take long for them to be moved through the barricade. Arthur had military contacts and his expertise had moved them through the line with relative ease. Aya watched the apocalypse happen from the relative safety of a military base. Her parents hovered round her like flies, keeping a watchful eye on her as they moved to fulfill the duties they felt were necessary to keep them safe and housed under the military's all-seeing gaze. Lila kept up with Aya's schooling whenever she could, and Aya didn't quite grasp how bad everything was until they weren't welcome in the base anymore.

They were given a payment as the government bought back their house and land when Arthur and Lila agreed that they had no intention of going back to the farm. They had accumulated hours of back pay and once life was settling down and getting back to normal, they were given another large payment and released from their duties as military consultants.

Aya was fourteen when they left the military base and began to reintegrate themselves into normal life.

Two years had given humanity enough time to get over the fact that the dead were rising and life had continued, partly thanks to the governments across the globe banding together and implementing 'zombie protocols' and partly because that's what humanity does - it survives. Weapons were legalized and open carry was commonplace. Pretty much everyone was welcome to own a gun, regardless of mental health. Protection from zombies was far more important than keeping mentally unstable individuals from shooting people. Walls were erected around interior neighbourhoods, communities that were partially government controlled, and some that were run by gangs and bands of neighbours who had gotten sick of the violence and uncertainty. The government decided that chain link fences were easy enough to rebuild and they walled off the cities, making checkpoints for anyone travelling between cities by car. Air travel was much more limited and checks were put in place for anyone going in or coming out.

Aya's parents debated long and hard about where they wanted to go, what was best for their family. Aya was happy to be away from the military and she prayed that her parents would agree. Eventually, they decided that it was their duty to stay in the city and help those they could. Rural living was nice, but the premiums on country properties had gone up since the zombies happened. More people wanted to live farther away from people in general, but no one wanted to give up the safety and convenience that the cities afforded. Eventually, Lila and Arthur agreed that the city was the best place for their family, Aya could learn better living in the city, and the military wouldn't tear apart an entire city block looking for them should their assistance be needed in the future. They bought a condo in a high rise, paying premium to get on a higher floor and to be sure that the building was top of the line when it came to security.

Arthur went back to working in the hospitals, his penance, he decided, for missing the beginning of the apocalypse when people were desperate for help. His work for the military had been top secret and he didn't speak to anyone about it, not even his wife. Whatever they had forced him to do, he never once said, only that he needed to help the people who he couldn't save and being a doctor and taking the risk of becoming infected by spontaneous outbreaks was everything that he needed to do.

When Aya was fourteen, the first Rapture aired.

Lila and Arthur were disgusted and shocked that the government would allow such a program to take place. They watched in mute horror as "lottery winners" were forced to survive in a secret location for three days with questionable supplies and shoddy morality. When the first contestant was killed, Lila sprang into action. Her voice would not stay silent. Arthur agreed and he helped to organize the protests around the Rapture, and Lila worked from home. The doctor and the sociologist became the loudest voices in the wake of the Rapture and soon, other people followed suit. For every sponsor the Rapture gained, another venue was added to the list of places that would refuse to air it. Lila used her clout to worm her way into the UN and the protests continued, though the Rapture refused to stop.

Lila was happy to stay at home with Aya, choosing to homeschool and teach her survival skills, rather than risking her daughter's life on a commute every day. Aya was more than happy to stay at home, and she excelled in her schooling, graduating at sixteen. A week after graduation, Lila decided that it was time to have a discussion with her daughter.

"We need to talk," Lila said as the Rapture was gearing up to begin again. She was sitting at the dining room table, drinking a mug of tea and looking far more tired than Aya had seen her look since her dad died suddenly of a heart attack in one of his lectures.

Aya nodded. "Is it the Rapture?"

"You're old enough to make your own decisions about it," Lila said, waving her hand to tell Aya to sit at the table. Aya obliged wordlessly. "You've seen this thing start when you were a child. You're old enough now to understand the implications of such a thing. If you don't want to work against it, you don't have to. I am not going to force my beliefs on you, and you're old enough to make up your own mind."

Aya smiled and reached across the table, patting her mother's hand affectionately. "Mom, you've raised me better than to think that I would condone the killing of innocent people for sport. I haven't forgotten what it was like when we were running away that first night. I've seen kids my age get thrown into the Rapture, and I've watched then die on national TV. Believe me, I don't like it, and I want it to stop. Just point me in the direction you want me to go and I'm gone."

Lila smiled back, the exhaustion in her face making her smile seem wan and thin. She nodded slowly. "You are the best daughter I could ever have asked for. Your father would be proud."

Aya nodded, resolute in her hatred for the Rapture, and determined to be a voice for change. She worked tirelessly alongside her mother, and independently from her, organizing her own protests and making her own connections. Aya was the voice for the younger crowd, the ones who were willing to speak up against the government. She built up bail funds for those who got arrested during their protests, and she was singlehandedly responsible for the initial creation of the ethics committee that oversaw the Rapture after their third year.

Aya Wu had become the loudest opponent of the Rapture and she'd garnered international attention for it. Between interviews on TV news during her protests, and her bi-weekly ration of tear gas during said protests, there was barely a person involved with the Rapture who didn't know her name.

Aya was well aware that she was going to become a target. She knew that the so-called lottery that picked names was less random than the Controllers claimed, and she always kept one eye open for anyone who looked suspicious while she was walking. One day, it would be inevitable that Aya would find herself on national TV again, but not for the reasons she would want.

She had resigned herself to knowing that she would eventually wind up as a contestant of the Rapture. And she prayed that, when it happened, the people she'd worked so tirelessly to inspire would rise up like the living dead and raise a little hell on her behalf.

At twenty-two, Aya Wu had become the loudest voice speaking up against the Rapture.

She'd put herself through college by working crappy jobs to pay for tuition. She'd become a city civil servant, working clean up when spontaneous outbreaks occurred, or when hordes broke through the walls that surrounded the city. The pay was good, but the work sucked and Aya never wanted to do it again if she could help it. She studied hard and trained for survival on the weekends. She had gotten used to the fact that she wasn't 'normal'. She didn't listen to music and she never wore high heels. She didn't party, and had very little interest in dating since most boys scoffed at her involvement with the anti-Rapture movement. She had never been to a salon to have her nails done, the girls she knew pitied her and always tried to convince her to come with them and get a manicure, she might like it, but Aya steadfastly refused. It was pointless for her to allow herself to have those luxuries. She was a girl, but she was the kind of girl who knew how to field dress a broken leg and stitch wounds on herself, and others, but not how to contour her makeup or walk in five inch stiletto heels. She had led more than one rescue mission when the failsafes in the national parks where people were dumb enough to go camping failed. She'd killed more than her fair share of the undead, though she'd never been able to bring herself to pull the trigger on someone who had been infected but not turned.

Aya Wu was lithe and muscular from her training and she wore her hair longer than was probably smart, but at least she kept it tied back. Her hair was the one thing she'd allow herself to have, and she took pride in the ebony locks that she'd inherited from her mother, though she'd never bothered to learn to style them outside of a braid or ponytail. She always wore running shoes or hiking boots and jeans and was the kind of girl to carry a pharmacy in her messenger bag.

The Controllers of the Rapture program knew her very well; she'd been under surveillance since the first day she'd protested against the use of zombies in game shows. Her skills with firearms and public speaking were a matter of public record, the Controllers wanted to make sure that they knew what they were getting into before Aya was dropped off into the wilds to face off against the zombie hordes, and the unstable players chosen for the Rapture. She was groomed to be an ethical killing machine, and the Controllers knew she would make for good television. Her staunch disapproval of the Rapture Program, and her stubborn willingness to survive no matter what would help her outlast the others, and if she died, it was no skin off anyone's teeth.

Aya was aware of the surveillance. She had learned how to pick out government agents at a hundred yards, and the Rapture Program's spies were even more obvious to her. She chatted them up, shared her lunch with them on more than one occasion and even brought them coffee when they were in public and looking out of place. It pained them to know that she was genuinely caring and that it wasn't just a front and anyone who expressed concerns over the legitimacy of what they were doing disappeared.

Aya never thought twice about it, she couldn't allow herself the pity. It was when the surveillance stopped and there was no one left obviously watching her that she began to worry. They had *always* been there, watching, waiting. The disappearance of the men who would track her every move spoke louder than the fact that they had been there at all. Aya tightened up her movements. She stopped going for coffee once a week. She didn't linger to chat, mumbling apologies. The closer the airdate of the Rapture got, the more paranoid Aya became.

She hadn't expected them to take her in broad daylight, and she certainly hadn't expected them to take her on the street.

The cart she had been pulling behind her and the groceries in it were left on the sidewalk, and Lila never did get to make the Sunday dinner she'd been planning.

CHAPTER THREE

Comedown

Aya's legs were still shaking as the drugs worked their way out of her system, but she didn't stop moving. She checked the house first; everything was exactly as she remembered it, two bedrooms on the main floor, a bathroom, the living room, laundry and kitchen. The carpet on the stairs had been replaced, and the kitchen had been updated. The master bedroom at the top of the stairs had been repainted and the closet extended. The attic space had been turned into an extension of the room, with new drywall and a new window. It was warm upstairs, the room had been turned into a luxurious master retreat, and the bed looked very inviting. Aya hesitated in the doorway, debating on actually getting into bed. It was a queen-sized mattress, piled high with designer pillows and comforters.

The sick feeling in her guts and the exhaustion leftover from the sedatives made it a very tempting prospect but Aya shook her head. She didn't want to risk sleeping on the job, and the blinking camera mounted on the wall made her uneasy. With a sigh, she turned away from the luxurious suite and continued on her way.

She checked the other two rooms. Next door to the master suite was another bedroom that had been updated, the wood panelling removed since the time she'd been there, and the floor updated. It had, at one point, served as her bedroom, her parents deciding to keep Aya close. It had since been renovated into a modern, grey guest room. There was very little personality in the room. Aya shuddered, pushing aside memories of playing in the wood panelled room, and moving on. At the other end of the small hallway, above the laundry room was another room. It had been Aya's playroom as a child, the built-in shelves had been reconfigured and the room had been painted into a muted shell pink and used for what looked to have been a craft room. The light hitting the window shone through and Aya put her hand against the wall as her kneed threatened to buckle. Childhood memories flooded her and she took the briefest of moments to steady herself before she hurried back down the stairs to head outside. According to her cell phone it was just after six in the morning, and she knew that the game started at nine. The sun was already above the horizon and she was afraid the day would be too hot for comfort, despite it being late August. The weather had been exceptionally hot all summer and while the nights were already sharp with the icy tang of autumn, Aya didn't want to have to do manual labour to fortify the house in sweltering heat. If there was one thing that she remembered clearly about the old farmhouse, it was how stifling and warm the entire thing got during the summer.

Aya wasted no time in checking the huge garden plot for vegetables. The larder had been partially stocked with canned goods and rice that she fully planned to eat, but she'd prefer it if she could save the canned stuff in case she had to bail. She found a few abandoned plants, but there were enough ripe vegetables for a couple of good meals. She pulled up the carrots, finding bright orange roots that made her mouth water. She grinned to herself and nodded. If the carrots were growing that meant the potato plants that were left would have at least a few that she could scavenge. It wouldn't be much, but with a can of soup it would make a better meal than she'd expected to find. The crab apple trees and the towering Saskatoon berry trees were full of ripe fruit, too, and she made a note to harvest some of it before she holed up.

The ground was as familiar to her as her own face and she found herself falling into an easy gait as she explored the farm that she had grown up on, until the apocalypse had forced her family to move away. Her old footpaths came back to her unbidden and she found herself following the same path she'd used to gather firewood as she tried not to let herself be overwhelmed by the fond memories of childhood. She walked past the house, turning the corner of the large yard and heading toward the old wood shed. She knew there was an outlying barn and another shed further ahead, the equivalent of a city block away from the house and out in the field, but the wood shed was where she knew she needed to go.

The shed was old, built when her grandparents had first lived on the farm, and the wood was thin and splintering. It wouldn't make for a good shelter if she was swarmed during the game, but she was praying to whichever God might be listening that the Controllers had left her something that she could work with. She reached out for the rusted handle on the shed and pulled the door. It stuck, just like she remembered it would and she repositioned her hand so she could lift the sagging door as she pulled it open.

Aya let out a low whistle as she laid eyes on the treasure the Controllers had left her. It was a weapons cache, and it was bigger than Aya had hoped. The thin shelves and drooping tables that had once been used to store root vegetables while they dried had been filled with various weapons. Guns, knives, a couple of tactical bags all gleamed in the dim light. There were a few hand tools lining the walls and a stack of plywood in the corner.

"Thank you," Aya whispered. She stepped into the shed and reached for a bag. She made her way carefully between the rows of tables, eyeing the guns suspiciously. She had a nagging feeling that these were dummy guns, that they'd jam or not have a firing pin. The Controllers would be thrilled if she was killed in The Rapture, her mom would be broken, and the protests would lose their leaders. She shook her head. That would be cheating, se decided. She reached for a handgun and popped the magazine out. It was fully loaded already. She slid the clip back in and stopped dead.

A rustling sounded outside and a shadow fell across the doorway. Aya set her bag down and levelled the gun at the door. She fingered the safety, taking it off. She had no intention of dying in a shed. She stepped forward quietly as the shadow grew longer, the footsteps outside slowing. Fingers appeared on the edge of the door, pulling it aside a little further. A face peered around the door.

"Don't. Move."

"Oh shit."

Aya stayed her trigger finger as the man spoke. At least he wasn't a zombie. He held his hands out in front of him as he moved around the edge of the doorway. Aya looked him over He was five-ten, in dusty jeans, hiking boots and a black T-shirt. His dirty blonde hair stuck up at all angles and he had a bit of scruff on his chin. He was slender, but the way his shirt clung to him proved he had some muscle definition. His blue eyes were wide and he was scared.

"Please don't shoot me," he said. "I'm sorry, I'll leave. I'll leave, I just... please don't shoot me."

"You alone?" Aya demanded.

The man nodded.

"You armed?"

"No."

Aya frowned, staring him down. He didn't look like he was carrying any kind of concealed weapon, but she didn't want to make a stupid mistake before the game even started.

"Where the hell did you come from?"

"I... walked here. Down the highway. I woke up in a town about ten kilometres from here?"

"You walked?"

"All night."

Aya shifted her weight, debating. She didn't exactly want to be alone, but she knew better than anyone not to trust the other players in the Rapture. He spoke again, as if he could read her mind, trying desperately to put her at ease, and his voice was cracked, tinged with exhaustion when he did.

"Please, I don't want to be here."

"No one does," Aya agreed. "What's your name?"

"Connor."

Aya sighed and lowered her gun, putting the safety back on. "Congratulations on winning the lottery."

"Fuck this," Connor replied with a shake of his head. "Thank you," he added, eyeing Aya over. "Are you alone, too?"

"Yeah. That's sort of how they run this. They don't expect people to team up, they want you to be paranoid and trigger happy."

"And are you?" Connor asked, eyeing the weapons.

"That's really up for debate," Aya replied. "You can lower your hands, Connor, I'm not going to shoot you."

Connor breathed an audible sigh of relief and let his hands drop harmlessly to his sides. He peered around the shed, taking it in fully for the first time, eyes widening as he did. "So... uh... are all these weapons yours?"

"Guess so," Aya said, turning her back on Connor and picking up the bag she'd dropped. Connor didn't move and Aya shot him a look over her shoulder. He was still standing in the doorway, looking for all the world like a lost puppy. He was dirty and sweaty and Aya swore that he was shaking a little bit. She wondered if she had spooked him. She stared openly at him, weighing him. She knew she'd be screwed if he had a knife, but he hadn't tried to attack her yet. She hated that she was even considering it, but he really didn't look like he was armed, and if Aya was going to be honest with herself, she really, truly didn't want to be alone in the house she'd grown up in, the house she'd been in when the apocalypse happened. It was too much and having another person around might make it easier to take. Ignoring the protest in her guts, she made a decision about the stranger standing in the door of her shed.

"Hey Connor? You know anything about shooting?"

"Aye," Connor replied, taking a hesitant step into the shed. "Who doesn't nowadays?"

"You'd be surprised about how many people are still uncomfortable around the sight of a gun," Aya explained, her tone casual as she checked each weapon she selected before dropping it, and the corresponding ammunition, into the bag. There were fifteen guns total, and Aya wasn't sure that she wanted to leave any, but she was less sure that she wanted to take all of them. "Do you prefer shotguns or handguns?"

"Rifles. I prefer long distance shooting. I grew up in a hunting family, and work often led me to using a rifle to snipe zombies on the walls of the neighbourhoods I was stationed in."

Aya frowned and nodded, impressed by his honesty and lack of bravado. Most men she'd posed the same question to, when faced with hordes of the undead in the 'real world' would put on a macho show for her and end up proving how little they knew about guns. She'd had her fair shares of close calls in the wilds of suburbia where zombie outbreaks still sometimes happened, and the people she'd ended up working with had claimed to know everything, but in practice fell short. Hearing Connor tell the truth was refreshing. "Fair enough. You want a handgun or two, too?"

"I wouldn't mind a sidearm, thanks. Are you actually gonna arm me?" Connor asked.

"I don't plan on shooting you, at this point and having an extra set of eyes and a guy who knows his way around a rifle could definitely come in handy," Aya agreed with a shrug. "If you want to stick around, anyway."

"I would love to stick around, thank you."

"Grab a bag, pick your guns, then we're fortifying the house using those sheets of plywood."

"Thank you," Connor said again, stepping into the small shed and moving toward the rifles. He touched each one before making his choices, picking each one up and giving it a look over. Aya watched him, impressed that he seemed to actually know what he was doing.

Her gut instinct was still to kick him out and let him get eaten, she couldn't trust anyone, not with the Controllers doing everything in their power to set her off her game psychologically. For all she knew, this guy was a spy, sent to distract her.

Despite it all, Aya really didn't want to face the Rapture alone.

"Hey Connor? You any good at chopping firewood?"

Connor grinned. "I'm not bad at it, why?"

Aya shot Connor a sideways look. "Do you always have to ask so many questions?"

"I figure that if we're going to be partners in this little venture, I should get to know you a bit, don't you think?"

"No."

"Why not?"

"People die in this event, Connor. I'm not entirely planning to make it out of here alive, and I'm sure that the Controllers wouldn't think of it as too much of a loss if I die."

Connor frowned and leaned against the table where he had been admiring the rifles. "Why would think like that?"

"There you go, asking questions again."

"No, really. That's not a good way to think," Connor insisted. "You're not going to die here, we're gonna get out of this."

Aya chuckled darkly. "You are far too optimistic to be here, my friend."

"Maybe," Connor agreed, "I still don't think you're gonna die."

"Not with you around?" Aya sneered, watching Connor for a reaction.

Colour crept into Connor's face and he ran a hand through his hair. "When you say it like that, I feel like a giant jackass."

Aya chuckled dryly. "But you were thinking it, weren't you?"

"I..." Connor paused. "I don't know what to think, but to be honest, you've already saved my life, so if I can repay the favour, I will."

Aya shrugged. "Get your guns, and let's get this show on the road. There's not much time before the event actually starts and I'm not about to get caught with my proverbial pants down. Again."

Connor nodded and did as he was told, following Aya back toward the house when she was satisfied with the amount of weaponry they could carry. They each put a handgun on their belts before going about the hard task of fortifying the house. They used the sheets of plywood to board up the windows on the main floor from the inside and hiding the side door with a strategically placed sheet of plywood and nails. Aya wasn't happy with it, but it was better than nothing, and at least the extra fortification would give them a few extra minutes to decide how to get out of the house if a horde of zombies showed up. Next, Aya asked Connor to chop firewood, and she showed him to the farther shed by the barn and told him to bring the axe back to the house when he was done. She went and gathered as much fresh food from the garden as she could store in the house without a fridge and set to work preparing it.

Connor arrived back to the house with a wheelbarrow full of firewood and enough kindling to get a decent fire started just as their wrist devices began beeping. "Shit," Connor breathed. "That's the half hour countdown. Where should I put this?"

Aya looked over at the front door, which led into the kitchen from a mudroom that had once been a kind of covered porch. The beeping of the device on her wrist didn't faze her, she'd been keeping track of the time and trying not to let the nausea she felt creeping up on her overwhelm her. "In the living room, I think. I don't want to be back and forth all night."

"You think there's enough here to keep the fire going the whole time?" Connor asked as he started to unload.

"With what's in the mudroom there should be," Aya agreed. "I think we can last the whole three days here if we're careful."

"What about food?"

"We're lucky, there was some canned stuff and I managed to scavenge a good amount from the garden. The water still works, even though the lights don't. There were some candles, too. That stove in the living room is perfect for cooking on, and there's pots in here that'll work to cook with."

"Lucky break indeed," Connor agreed, dusting off his pants and shirt as he walked back into the kitchen. He set the axe down on the floor next to the cupboards where Aya could see it. "You sure we're gonna be safe here?"

"No."

"Well, do you think we've got enough of everything to last for three days?"

"No."

"Is there anything you do know for sure?"

"No, sorry. They like to do everything in their power to throw us off, remember? I wouldn't be surprised if the water from the well has been laced with sedatives and the canned stuff in the cupboards is intentionally expired with the intent of giving us food poisoning and slowing us down even more. Drama like that makes for good television."

Connor frowned. "You act like you've been through this before."

Aya sighed and set down the knife she was using to chop garden vegetables. "No. I've never been through this, but I've seen enough of these events to know where it's going. I've studied them extensively, I know how the

Controllers think, and I try my damnedest to keep one step ahead of them, or at least to think worse than them. My name is Aya Wu. My family..."

"Are the most well-known activists speaking out against the Rapture since its inception," Connor finished, mouth agape. "I know who you are. I'm sorry, I thought it might have been when I first met you, but I just wasn't sure if that was really you. I mean... wow. That's a ballsy move by the Controllers, aye? I mean, it's not like you're just some dumb schmuck off the streets. You're high profile. You're kind of a celebrity, and huge influence on me... and I just... I still can't quite believe that I'm really standing here talking to you, that it's really you."

"Yeah, it's really me," Aya spat. "So no, I haven't been through this before, but I've been prepared for this for a long time. I've always sort of half-expected this to happen. I just wasn't expecting this to happen now."

Connor nodded, running a hand through his hair in a nervous gesture. "So what are you going to do?" he asked after a long moment. "I mean, you've gotta have some sort of plan right? Someone like you, you said that you've been expecting this to happen one day right? So you've gotta have some courageous plan to get the hell out of here? Something to take down the system from the inside?"

Aya laughed. "You've seen far too many movies, Connor. No. I'm staying here. This is my home; this is the house I lived in when the apocalypse happened. I haven't been back here since the zombies first rose. It's been ten years or so? I'm surprised that this place hasn't burned down. Bastards thought they'd drop me here to try and break me. It's a tactic to unnerve me. Everything about this is a plot to get me to break, or to participate."

"You don't want to participate?"

"I didn't kill you, did I?" Aya pointed out.

Connor shifted his weight. "No. You didn't. You probably should have."

"Why?"

Connor shrugged. "Teaming up with a completely random stranger doesn't seem like a very good tactic."

"You're here, teaming up with me. Don't you think you should take your own advice?"

"No," Connor admitted. "I can't not have someone watching my back. I'm no good that way. I don't function as well, or as efficiently on my own. I mean, I ran down the highway, completely unarmed and not knowing where I was going. I'm not the smartest tool in the shed."

Aya grinned at the sentiment. "You a little paranoid, there, Conn?"

"Not really, mostly running on instinct."

"So then why would you think that I would want to kill you?"

"I don't think you'd kill me intentionally anymore," he admitted. "But at first? I scared you. You were armed. You had every right to shoot me and no one could hold it against you. Now? If you were gonna kill me, I think you'd do it so that you can win."

"I don't want to win," Aya said. "I want to survive and get the hell out of here. I will not give these bastards the chance to profit from my participation. You can leave if you want," she offered. "I don't expect you to follow me in this decision. Take some food, take some guns and have at it, if you want."

Connor reached a hand out and placed it over Aya's. "I appreciate the offer, but I think I'm gonna ride this one out with you, if you don't mind."

Aya nodded. "Thanks."

"What do you want me to do?"

"Make sure we've fortified everything we can, and set up a lookout spot in one of the upstairs rooms. I'm gonna finish preparing these vegetables, then I'll start a fire and cook them, and after lunch, we'll make a better plan."

Connor nodded again, snapping a messy, two fingered salute before hurrying off to do as Aya asked. Aya sighed and went back to finishing the vegetables. It was going to be a long three days.

CHAPTER FOUR

Let the Games Begin

Lunch was sparser than Aya had hoped to make it, but she wasn't willing to risk stretching their rations thinner than she absolutely had to. She'd boiled potatoes and carrots together with a handful of other vegetables she'd brought in from the garden. There was no milk or butter, but there had been some salt left behind, and that was good enough for her. She chose to save the canned soups for supper, and for when they ran out of fresh food. It would be easier to transport a can of spaghetti and a can of stew than a bunch of potatoes. If Connor was unhappy with the Spartan meal, he didn't complain and the two ate in tense but companionable silence. The stove was warm, but didn't give off much light and the sound of cutlery against chipped bowls filled the spaces between the crackling fire.

"Did you see anyone else while you were running?" Aya asked as she settled herself in front of the stove. The drugs working their way out of her system left her feeling shaky and cold and she didn't like it.

Connor shook his head. "I was dumped in the open, like they didn't want me to get past the first couple of hours."

"They're a bunch of bastards," Aya agreed. "But they claim there's no danger until the countdown is over. Supposedly it's to make sure that everyone recovers from being drugged before the games actually start."

"They don't mean most of what they say, do they?"

"It's a load of shit, to be honest."

Connor nodded. "I was in a backyard. There was a sliding glass door, and I went into the house because I was confused as hell. I mean, I was at a party in Nottingham North last night, so waking up in a backyard with a headache isn't entirely unheard of."

"So you ran?"

"Well, I drank some water from the tap before I realized that I had no idea where I was."

Aya snorted a laugh. "And then your phone didn't work?"

"I didn't have my phone at all."

"That sucks, I'm sorry."

Connor shrugged. "The landline didn't work either. No lights. This fucking thing," he held up the wrist that had the bracelet on it, "was what clued me in to where I was and what had happened. I broke a few things in my rage and then decided that I wasn't going to risk staying in the city."

"And you didn't see anyone?"

"No. But I heard what sounded like fighting. Breaking stuff, things getting knocked over, gunfire. You know, normal sounds to hear in a zombie apocalypse," he shrugged. "The gunfire wasn't something I wanted to contend with and there were no weapons to be had anywhere, so I ran the hell out of the town. I thought I'd have better luck away from the fighting."

"And then you found out that you're in the sticks in the ass crack of nowhere."

"I didn't say it was a very good plan."

"At least you tried," Aya teased. "Best laid plans and all that."

"So what about you? This is it for your plan, huh?" Connor asked as he set his empty bowl aside. "Just sit here and eat mashed potatoes for three days?"

"I was thinking about dragging the mattress down from the room upstairs and building a pillow fort, too," Aya replied.

"What if something happens? You know how this program goes."

Aya shrugged. "Do you know what a Bug Out Bag is?"

"Kind of, I've never really had the need for one though."

"Well, we're each going to make one with those bags we brought in."

"Why?"

"Because this is The Rapture. You know damn well how this program goes." Aya stared at Connor. "And what do you mean you've never had the need for one?"

"I live in a gated community," Connor offered by way of explanation. "Nottingham North."

Aya grew very still and quiet. "Sorry."

Gated communities were both a luxury and a disaster since the apocalypse began. Most were government-run or military based. Walls had been erected around abandoned communities that hadn't been too damaged in the initial clean up of the first zombie outbreaks. Houses were cleaned, quarantined and checked out for anything that might spread viruses, such as contaminated water or air conditioners that had been broken or otherwise contaminated, before people were moved back in. There had been a huge clamour to get into these so-called safe communities. People had rioted and petitioned, and eventually, the military had to step in to keep things from getting out of hand. The government began making mandates about who could get into a gated community. The walled suburbs had very strict rules about what could and could not happen within the walls of the communities, and populations were closely monitored. The goings-on inside those walls were hush-hush, each community had its own set of rules, regulations, and a sort-of informal internal governing system, and armed guards monitored it all. Eventually, illegal gated communities sprung up across the country, and the clamour died down. The government allowed it because it meant that if an outbreak happened inside one of the non-government communities, there wouldn't be any news coverage and clean up would be simple. Getting your family into a government controlled gated community, however, was a feat in and of itself, and getting out of one would take nothing short of a miracle.

"I didn't know that gated communities were scoured for Rapture contestants," Aya admitted.

Connor snorted. "I'm from Nottingham North. It's essentially becoming a ghetto behind walls where military men wander back and forth, shooting first and asking questions later. It's the old tenements you read about in the history books, the Irish are packed away there to die."

"Is that true?"

"Nottingham North is mostly Irish immigrants," Connor agreed. "Has been since the apocalypse started. I think we have one black neighbour and one Russian family, but the rest of us are Irish stock. It's fun on St. Paddy's, that's for sure," he smiled fondly at the memory, his happy-go-lucky optimism wavering for the briefest of moments. "I mean, I figure they're all kind of like that, right? There are a couple of gated communities in what used to be Harlem that are black communities. I just assumed that they were all the same?"

"You said 'we' didn't you?" Aya asked. "Girlfriend?"

Connor grinned. "Brother, actually."

"How did you end up in a gated community?" Aya asked. "My family didn't get into one, and we tried."

Connor shifted his weight. "Well, we're former IRA, and all things considered about Nottingham, being former IRA, well, that comes with a few perks, y'know?"

"Former?"

Connor shook his head. "That's a story for a different time."

Aya nodded. "Coffee after this is all over, then."

"I'd definitely like that," Connor agreed. "So you're not planning on dying here anymore?"

"Not if I can help it," Aya confided with a nod. "But I'm sure as hell not participating. I refuse to have my name sullied and put on lunch boxes to make a buck for the Corporation."

"I hear that," Connor agreed, shooting a pointed look into the camera mounted on the wall above them. "I'm sure they do, too."

"They've probably bugged my phone, too," Aya complained. "Won't be surprised if we hear a recording of my last phone call to my mom on the intercoms to wake us up tomorrow."

"You think they'd do that?"

"I wouldn't put it past them."

"You really think they have it out for you?"

Aya fixed Connor with an unamused look. "They think that I'm going to fight, going to kill whoever it takes and do whatever it takes to get myself out of here. They don't want me to make an even bigger name for myself. They don't want me to be immortalized or canonized. If I die, I'm a martyr and my cause explodes, my mom, if they don't assassinate her, will rally people. The Corporation won't be able to justify the Rapture anymore. If I participate, I become a star and they use me as a marketing tool. If I don't do a damn thing, they can't hoist me up and put me on a pedestal. If I make it through the three days, there's nothing they can do about it."

"They can leave you."

"They're recording everything right now, remember? I'm a star, sort of. At least, everyone watching knows who I am. And if they don't, they probably do now."

"So that's your plan? Sit it out and wait?"

Aya shrugged and looked at the cuff on her wrist. "We've been here for four hours since the start of the event. I figure that we can..."

Aya's eyes went wide as her words trailed off. Connor was on his feet before Aya could say anything. They had both heard distant popping, like fireworks. Aya pulled herself to her feet and drew her sidearm as Connor opened the living room side door. They slipped into the cool mid-afternoon air; the weather hadn't warmed up as much as Aya had thought it would, as another loud popping echoed across the flat expanse of land around the farmhouse.

"What the hell is that?" Aya asked. "Fireworks?"

"No, that was an improvised explosive," Connor replied.

"How can you tell?"

Connor shot Aya a pointed look and raised his eyebrows. Aya nodded in understanding and she followed Connor as he moved from the shelter of the line of pine trees that stood sentinel and hid the side door from the curved driveway. They stopped in the driveway as another, louder explosion echoed through the air.

"That was something bigger," Connor muttered as he took off running.

Aya followed as Connor sprinted down the dirt road and to the highway that ran past the farm. He stopped and Aya skidded to a halt next to him, nearly running into him as he pointed. A huge billowing black cloud rose above the tree line.

"That's from town," Aya muttered. "Is that the mill?"

"How many gas stations are there in that town?" Connor asked.

"Two, I think?" Aya replied. "I mean, I haven't been here for ten years, and I was twelve when we left, it could be more now. Maybe three?"

"That'll be from the gas station, I'd wager."

Aya was about to answer when another explosion rocked the silence of the world. Louder, this time, and more smoke began to billow into the sky.

"Well, at least we know where the other contestants are?" Connor suggested.

Aya shook her head. "That's the bigger of the two towns around here," she explained, pointing. "We're currently sitting about halfway between the two. If you go that way," she pointed in the opposite direction, "and just follow the highway, you'll go down a big hill and come to a valley and find yourself in a tiny hamlet. One corner store, one gas station attached to that corner store. A bar. A hotel. A restaurant. Some houses. It's only there because logging trucks and freight trucks use this highway and need places to refuel and rest. If you keep going, there's another town about twenty minutes by car, and I'll bet you any money we can't get there because they've set up the perimeter just on the other side of the valley through that town."

Connor nodded. "Yeah, I woke up on the edge of the perimeter, in a backyard. The perimeter is a fence and it's like right outside of town on the other side."

"Fuck," Aya replied, running her hands through her hair. "We're fucked."

Connor shrugged. "Look, we'll make it out of here," he promised, casting a worried glance over at the billowing clouds of smoke still rising from the town he'd woken up in. "I'm kinda glad I ended up here instead of sticking around in town."

Aya nodded and patted his arm. "Come on, we still have to build our Bug Out Bags."

"You don't think we're going to be able to stay here, do you?"

"I'd rather have them ready and not need them, than need them and not have them. I've seen what happens if you're not prepared, and

I'm not willing to get eaten by a horde of zombies, or starve and get sluggish when I can't find food."

Connor nodded and followed Aya back into the house. They locked the door as another explosion sounded.

"That's three."

Aya shrugged. "We're not going that way if we can help it."

"What do you want to put in these bags?"

Aya sighed. "Ammo, food, water. First-aid supplies if we have any. Knives, tools, matches."

"Rope?"

"Did you find some?"

Connor nodded.

"Sure. Might come in handy."

Connor chuckled. "My brother never thought so, but we always ended up needing it."

"Hold that thought," Aya said, disappearing into the kitchen. Connor grabbed his bag and settled himself back on the floor near the stove while he waited. He could hear Aya rummaging through the contents of the kitchen, debating on what to bring. She returned in a few minutes, arms full of various cans, a can opener dangling from her fingers. Connor got up and relieved her of some of the burden before settling himself back down.

"Sounds like you two had some wild adventures."

Connor shrugged and unzipped the bag he'd chosen, taking the ammunition and guns out to rearrange the contents. His hand lingered on the rolled up rope he'd found before setting it on the floor with the rest of his possessions. "You could say that."

"Is he dead?" Aya asked. "Is that why you're so hesitant to talk about him?"

"No. I'm just trying to process the fact that I might not see him again. Don't want to linger too much on that thought. We're close, you know? Best friends, always had each other's backs. Not even girls would get between us, it just didn't work that way."

Aya frowned and took a seat on the floor, nodding, but saying nothing.

"Then the apocalypse happened, and I swear we were the best at what we were doing. We were on the front lines of clean up, search and rescue, everything that you don't normally associate with criminal organizations like the IRA? That sort of shit. We didn't break laws unless we had a reason, and we always had back up," he took a deep breath, shrugged and shook his head. "Things went south, shit that I can't talk about happened... We lost friends, and then we lost our collective nerves."

"And that didn't sit well with your employers?"

"You mean the Army? Not really, but they weren't going to kick us to the curb."

"I thought you said you were former IRA?"

"Loosely speaking, I'm a 'former' member of the IRA. I'm not doing anything active right now. Been mostly trying to..." he heaved another long and defeated sigh. "Never mind, it's not important. What's important is that I'm here, my brother isn't. I'm hoping that he's watching and that he can hear me, because I'm pissed as punch and if I make it out of here, there's a very long laundry list of jobs we're going to have to consider."

Aya shot a pointed look up over her own shoulder and at the camera intentionally placed in a place they would see it. "I'm sure they can hear you, and I'm sure the world is watching."

Connor nodded. "So, we're just packing supplies in these bags?" he asked, changing the subject.

"Enough to get us through three days, just in case we have to bolt."

"What about bottled water?"

Aya shook her head. "Don't have any."

Connor sighed. "Better hope that nothing bad is gonna happen to make us bolt, then."

Aya zipped up her bag, satisfied with what she'd packed. "Don't worry, Connor, I'm hoping."

If Connor noticed the edge in her voice and the lack of confidence that Aya was feeling, he didn't say anything. He nodded in return and forced a faux confident smile. As long as they were together, it was almost a believable like that they'd be okay.

CHAPTER FIVE

Connor

"Why the hell do you always volunteer us to go over the wall whenever anything remotely bad happens?"

Connor grinned to himself as he repositioned his body to make lying on his stomach more comfortable. His breath crystallized in front of him in little puffs that made him long for a cigarette and he swallowed the craving. He hadn't smoked in years, not since the dead started walking around and eating people, but every now and then the cravings would come back, like muscle memory in response to stress and fear.

"No, but seriously," Mac continued, his voice a harsh whisper in Connor's ear. "What the hell is wrong with you, Conn? You got some kinda death wish?"

Mac was a year younger than Connor, with darker hair and the same, sharp blue eyes. His face was softer than Connor's, with baby fat still in his cheeks, but the crow's feet around his eyes made him seem older, and more stern, than he was.

The brothers were hidden outside the confines of the city walls, well beyond the reach of Nottingham North, the walled community the Irish had taken over when the zombies had first arrived. It was a cold pre-autumn evening and they were bundled up against the chill in the air, huddled against the ground. Connor was on his stomach, peering through the scope of his rifle, looking for signs of the undead, and potentially, the living. Mac was complaining, breathing into his cupped hands and trying not to fall asleep.

They had helped build the community from the ground up, labouring to ensure that the families living within would be safe and well cared for. The IRA had been mobilized in America once the dead began rising. They were on the front lines of the clean up and containment while the rest of the citizens went apeshit, looting and rioting, or panicking and hiding. Mac and Connor had been inactive for a long time, having given up their street thug life in exchange for freedom, living in low rent housing and working minimum wage jobs, but at least they weren't doing anything illegal. Connor had long since lost his taste for living by the sword, and Mac, reluctantly, followed suit. Fifteen years of service, working for illegal organizations throughout high school just to ensure that they had a place to live, had taken its toll on Connor. His morals were shaky at best, and while he wouldn't hesitate to put the beating on anyone who he felt deserved it, he wasn't willing to do it for the money anymore.

The zombie apocalypse had been a blessing in disguise for the brothers. They were living in a run down apartment on the edge of the territory that would eventually become Nottingham North. When the dead started coming back to life, it didn't take long for the brothers to spring into action, rounding up the neighbours, most of who were elderly and single parents with young children, and herding them up to the safety of the upper apartments. They were armed, as all good IRA members would be, and set about the daunting task of holding off hordes of the undead at their doorsteps.

The neighbourhood they lived in was rough, partially gang controlled, and filled with low-income housing. It was a ghetto made up of immigrants from Ireland and other parts of Europe. It wasn't the nicest place, or the easiest to live, but it was their neighbourhood, and Connor and Mac would be damned if they were going to let their neighbours with young families get eaten by the living dead.

Connor went outside to defend the apartment, guns by his sides, trying to ignore the horrible task that Mac had assigned himself. Connor was always the softer, more sensitive one, better suited for diplomacy and his silver tongue had yet to fail him. Connor had always been the one who had trouble pulling the trigger. He wasn't the best at coming up with plans, but he would do as he was told, and he would do anything to avoid a fight if he could, able to talk his way out of more close calls than he could remember, and it had earned him a reputation as someone who could diffuse a situation and avoid unnecessary bloodshed. He was kind and gentle, where Mac had adopted the hard and hot-headed attitude that had saved his life on more than one occasion running errands for their bosses.

Connor felt his heart hammering in his chest as he walked down the stairs and away from the apartments where their neighbours had holed up at their behest. He could hear Mac talking softly to the people they were desperate to save, and the first broken sobs of heartbreak when the truth came out. Connor walked stiffly, forcing himself to keep his eyes ahead, to stay focussed on the task at hand and to hurry outside. They were mostly safe in the apartment building, so long as zombies couldn't climb stairs. Connor hid himself behind a low decorative wall in a basement stairwell to wait, guns ready for when the undead inevitably came knocking. He wasn't waiting long, and he fought off the horde until his ammunition ran out, and he ducked back inside to give Mac a report and figure out what they were going to do about the situation.

Mac refused to talk about what he had to do, but the apartment was safe while the rest of the world fell apart. The brothers agreed that they would protect the remaining people in their apartment, and that barricading themselves inside the building would be the smartest move, so long as water and power held out. They took turns raiding other buildings, looking for supplies and survivors while the other held off the zombie horde and kept an eye out for anyone that wasn't undead. They made good progress, collecting canned and dried goods from the tenements that had been abandoned in the initial panic, and they weren't worried about rationing right away. There were fewer mouths to feed after the first day, and Connor tried not to think about it when he prepared the evening meals.

The neighbourhood was one of the first ones to be called as a 'hot zone' when the dead began to take over the city. The people in Connor's care were written off as casualties of a war that no one had seen coming. The elderly, the immigrants, the poor single parents, they were the ones forgotten when the power went out and the moans of the undead filled the night air.

Connor and Mac never wavered in their diligence to the people they'd promised to take care of, and when the IRA returned to help clean up and check on their assets, the brothers were the first ones to willingly sign back up in exchange for help.

Nottingham North was one of the first walled communities, built mostly on Connor and Mac's sweat and blood, and initially filled with the people from their neighbourhood. The walls went up just beyond the tenements, and the people in the buildings were moved to the houses away from the rotting neighbourhood where the dead zombies were left to rot further. Nottingham was on the Northern edge of the city, a suburb beyond the reaches of the low-income area that has once been filled with fairly well to do people but now overrun with the dead. Connor and Mac had no hesitation to help their former bosses clean up the place and make it a safe area for their people. They didn't fill up every house and there were always rooms available for stragglers, as long as someone was willing to go and get them.

"We've been doing this for how many fucking years?" Mac asked again, breathing into his cupped hands. "The apocalypse started, what? Ten years ago?'

"Shh," Connor mumbled through gritted teeth as he tried to steady his shaking hands. He was cold. There were rumours of an outbreak five kilometres from Nottingham North, and someone needed to go and check it out. Survivors were always showing up in the midst of outbreaks, people who were otherwise displaced and roughing it, or idiots who forgot that the apocalypse had happened and decided that camping might be fun.

"You still trying to save yourself from eternal damnation by saving other people?" Mac continued, though all the antagonistic tones had left his voice. "You know, there's better ways to do that."

"You still think you're not just copying me to buy your own way into heaven?" Connor teased back, eyes never leaving the field below.

"Heaven doesn't exist for guys like us," Mac pointed out.

"That's the Catholic in you talking," Connor assured his brother.

Mac snorted and rubbed his hands together. "But seriously, why th' fuck do you always volunteer us to do these runs? How many people have we actually saved?"

"We've brought two dozen people home," Connor replied, "but only fifteen of them weren't infected."

"So just over half," Mac muttered. "And yet here we are, what's the point?"

Connor sniffled and shifted his weight, trying to get comfortable. "It's better than the alternative."

"What alternative."

Connor hesitated for a long moment before turning his head to look at his brother. "I'm not going back to the way it was before."

Mac snorted. "You know it's kill or be killed these days, right?"

"I'm not working for them anymore," Connor replied adamantly, pushing the bounds of petulance. "Not like we used to."

"So what? This is your way of keeping us in their good graces?"

"Something like that."

"We could just walk out of Nottingham, you know."

"You of all people should know that you don't just turn and walk away from these kinds of people, Mac."

Mac eyed his brother, running a hand across his chin as he did. "You don't trust them?"

"I don't trust anyone anymore."

"Do you trust me?"

"With my life."

"So what's got you all prickly about this all of a sudden?"

Connor grunted and pushed himself up onto his knees and off the cold ground. He knelt next to Mac, his rifle still pointed and ready to go in case of any signs of life. "Between you and me?"

"Always," Mac assured him with a curt nod.

"Have you seen the Rapture?"

"Aye. It's that god-awful game show they do every other year right? Ten people fucking get dumped in the middle of nowhere and are forced to kill or be killed while there's a bunch of zombies dicking around and it's all filmed."

"That's the one."

Mac hesitated. "What about it?"

Connor shook his head. "What kind of sick bastard comes up with that sort of concept?"

"Someone with too much money and a sadistic, psychotic streak?"

"That's a given."

"So what about it?" Mac asked. "You know the Army has nothing to do with that shit. At least, not directly."

"Well, I don't know that for sure," Connor replied. "But that's beside the point. I've been following it for the last couple years. Kinda gotten involved in some of the counter protests."

"Yeah, I know, I was there when you were washing the tear gas outta your eyes. Idiot, you're supposed to use milk."

"Okay, I'll remember that for next time, but why is it even a show? Why does anyone get chosen? Why isn't it just criminals getting thrown into a death match? Why is this even a thing that can make millions of dollars every time?"

"Are you saying you wanna get in on this game show thing, Conn?" Mac asked. "I mean, Lord knows we could use the money, but it's not like you're just gonna get up and picked."

"No, I don't want to get picked for the fucking Rapture," Connor argued. "I'm saying that why hasn't been stopped yet?"

"Money talks," Mac replied with a shrug. "You win some, you lose some, and the poor bastards who get picked up in the middle of the night and carted off to some demilitarized zone to fight zombies with shitty weapons and no food are definitely not on the winning side of things."

"What would you do if I was picked up and carted off in the middle of the night?" Connor asked.

"I'd raise holy hell."

"So why aren't you raising holy hell about it right now?"

Mac frowned. He'd fallen right into Connor's trap. He let out a low growl of frustration. "You and yer goddamn, bleeding heart bullshit, Conn! It's not right, I agree. It's sick and shouldn't be happening but what the hell can we do about it, huh? Ask the Army to get involved? Ha, they're probably fucking getting kickbacks from the guys in charge just to make sure that there's additional security in place and that no one crashes it. All we can do is hope that we're not the unlucky bastards who get picked, keep our heads down, and do what the bosses want as much as we can."

"And if that means going over the walls to find hordes of zombies, or rescue some drunken frat boys from getting eaten, then that's what I'm gonna keep doing."

"You're an ass," Mac grumbled. "You're never gonna get picked for the Rapture, Conn. You'd be too much of a hassle. You know your way around guns and fightin' zombies."

"They've got my face on camera from protests," Connor replied. "You never know."

"You're not that much of a pain in anyone's ass but mine," Mac grunted. "Now shut up and get back into position. There's a horde supposed to be coming this way and I don't wanna get caught off guard."

"Your optimism never fails to astound me," Connor muttered.

"And your idiocy never fails to annoy me," Mac replied, giving his brother a good-natured shove. "Let it go, brother. The Rapture doesn't happen to guys like us."

CHAPTER SIX

Controllers

The bullpen, a pile of computer monitors, television equipment and the technicians who ran it all, was alive with the hum of panic as alarms rang from several monitors. Screens flashed and machines beeped. Technicians ran around, trying to stop the myriad of alarms, and others manned camera stations, trying to stay out of the way of the people in charge of the alarms, while still trying to get everything that was happening on film through the CCTVs that had been placed in the battlefield for The Rapture.

"City cams three, nine and seventeen are compromised."

"City cams ten and thirteen are running, fifteen has a cracked lens, and is running but cuts out every few minutes."

"Turn off City cam fifteen, then. It was in the explosion, it's not important anymore."

"Where the *hell* are the other players?"

"Only Aya Wu hasn't moved, all other players have moved from the original drop-off points."

"Shit, shit, shit. Hordes two and six have been completely neutralized."

"City Two cams are all functional, but we've seen nothing happen so far."

Above it all, on a narrow catwalk overlooking the entire process, the Lead Controller stood watching the chaos with an impassive look on his face. The Lead Controller was a man named Alphonse Ritter. He had been on the original committee who introduced The Rapture to the world. He was a self-made millionaire, one of the richest men in the world. He hailed from Germany but had called America his home since long before the rising of the zombies. He had poured hundreds of thousands of dollars into ensuring that the Rapture was able to happen in the first place, and it was his savvy marketing skills that drew in enough sponsors to keep it running, even when ratings were down. He had pushed for the Rapture to be a yearly event, much to chagrin of the other original creators. They had pushed for it to remain once every five years, to avoid taking away from the importance of things like the Olympics, and Alphonse had pushed back.

Everyone wanted to know why he wanted to make it yearly. The Oscars and award shows that drew in so much money were yearly, why couldn't the Rapture be, too? His argument had been that the general population would respond well to the yearly stimulus of potentially being chosen for The Rapture. He argued that people would be more fit, more willing to take care of themselves if there was a yearly chance that they'd be chosen. Even when the government stepped in to make it bi-annual, money talked and Ritter got his way.

Alphonse was thin and muscular, well dressed in a Versace suit that drew attention away from his salt and pepper hair and the scars on his cheek that looked suspiciously like teeth marks. Whispers happened whenever Alphonse Ritter was around, and most of those whispers said that he had been bitten by a zombie but had somehow survived the infection. Other whispers suggested that he had the cure, but it was a temporary thing, and that he had to inject himself with antibiotics the way a diabetic must do with insulin.

Alphonse Ritter ignored the whispers. He let the common folk talk and paid them no mind. Idle chatter was the last thing that he needed to worry about.

Footsteps echoed across the metal grating that made up the catwalk as Alphonse's assistant, a severe-looking woman with blood red hair braided down her back, approached him. He eyed her casually, barely paying her heed as she stopped next to him. She was dressed in a pseudo-military style suit, and her posture suggested years of military training that hadn't quite been undone by civilian life.

"Have you seen the reports up close, Herr Ritter?" she drawled, holding out a manila folder.

"I don't think that I need to," Alphonse replied. "I can watch them all from here, but I assume that you'll feel better if you give me a run down of what's going on anyway, won't you, Hilda?"

"This game is different from any other one we've hosted before, sir," Hilda replied. "You may have been too reckless with the choices this year."

"Do you think so?" Alphonse asked, leaning forward and resting his elbows on the railing. "Do you think that this makes things more difficult than they need to be?"

"Do you want my opinion as your assistant?" Hilda asked. "Or do you want my opinion as someone who has seen first-hand experience in the face of zombie hordes?"

Alphonse smiled and looked at Hilda. She was in her late thirties, and had been Alphonse's assistant for seven years, having come into his service just before the Rising had happened. She was KGB and military trained and had studied analytics and business in school before joining the military in Germany. She was smart as a whip and merciless when it came to making business deals, and even more ruthless when it came time to do dirty work of all sorts. She had saved Alphonse's life more times than he could count, from everything from assassination in the business world, to zombie attacks. She had never failed him and he trusted her more than he had ever trusted anyone.

"I want your opinions in all aspects of your expertise," Alphonse replied after a long moment. "You can speak freely around me, you should know this by now."

"Then I think that bringing Aya Wu into this mix was a bad idea."

"Why?"

"She's a wild card," Hilda said without hesitation. "She is unpredictable, and the public's response to her abduction has not been favourable for us."

"I don't care what the public thinks."

"Viewership is down across the boards."

"Even in Russia?"

"No. It's up by two percent from last year."

Alphonse looked at Hilda. "So it's not all bad news."

"There are protests in markets in China, India and Canada. The Swiss are not happy that you've selected Aya, and they are calling for a stop to this year's games. The United Nations is getting involved."

"How long will they take to act on anything?" Alphonse asked with a nonchalant shrug. "By the time they get it together enough to do anything about it, the games will be over and Aya Wu will either emerge victorious, or be dead somewhere within the Rapture. Either way, we capitalize on it."

"If she dies, we'll be shut down, permanently."

Alphonse shook his head. "I don't think so."

"Her mother will cause a riot."

"She isn't that important, Hilda. What's important is that this game goes off without a hitch this year. What's important is that we get the ratings back up. Aya Wu doesn't matter to us. If she dies, she becomes a martyr and we use that to our advantage. If she wins, she becomes a hero and we market her as such. Let her preach about the evils of our game, people will pay to come see her speak."

"If I may be completely honest, Herr Ritter," Hilda interrupted, "I don't think that Aya Wu is the biggest concern of ours anymore."

"Who did we manage to piss off?"

"The IRA."

Alphonse chuckled and shook his head. "It's that damn Mick from Nottingham, isn't it?"

"His brother has reached out to the IRA. They are not happy."

"Well he ended up befriending Aya, I don't think we have much to worry about with the IRA. He'll survive, even if we have to rig the game to ensure it, just to keep the rest of them off our backs."

"There's one more thing I feel the need to mention."

Alphonse sighed. "If you're going to tell me about the two fucking pyromaniacs in City One..."

"No, sir," Hilda interrupted. "While it's unfortunate that they've managed to completely destroy two of the hordes that we had drugged up and waiting, they aren't the biggest cause for concern. They have been on the move, scouring the rest of City One, for what? We can't say, they've stopped talking aloud and it's becoming more difficult to translate what their gestures mean. They've been avoiding cameras as much as they can when they're talking and their hand signals are nonsensical. They seem to be laying low since they set off their IEDs in the gas stations and in the school where we had been keeping horde six. They haven't made another large scale move yet, but we're monitoring their movements. So far, they seem to be sleeping. I think that one of them is not reacting well to the drugs we used to get him here."

Alphonse grunted and fell silent. The Rapture had a dozen contestants every time. So far, he had heard of four of them, and so far none of it had been particularly good news. The contestants were chosen "randomly" in the public eye, but each year the contestants were specifically handpicked to be a volatile combination of people who were thought to make the best of the situation and who would provide the most drama. The ratings were always highest when he participants didn't get along, and betrayed each other at every available opportunity. So far, Alphonse had seen them pair off. Connor had found Aya and she hadn't killed him, and the two men in City One seemed to be getting along far better than anticipated.

"Then if they aren't the problem?"

"It's Agent Seven."

Alphonse groaned under his breath. "Son of a bitch. What happened to Agent Seven?"

Agent Seven was a codename given to one of the contestants chosen for The Rapture. He had been chosen specifically to counter Aya's pacifist ways. Where Aya was meant to be a sacrifice, Agent Seven was meant to be a ratings boost. Agent Seven had been the seventh person chosen for the contest, hence the name. He was not entirely sane, and Alphonse had known that when he'd chosen him. No one knew much about him, except that Agent Seven was a former inmate at a corrections facility. He was never officially charged with murder, but he was never officially cleared, either. He was one of those cases who had fallen through the cracks after the zombies had risen. Agent Seven had spent time in prison, before being shipped off to a mental institution for further treatment, and then back to a maximum security prison where most of his time had been spent in solitary. That maximum-security prison was where Alphonse had found him. Papers got shuffled, money likely changed hands, though no one would admit to it, and he eventually fell through the cracks and ended up on the streets. He'd ended up in New Orleans, living in what most people referred to as a 'feral colony' and fighting zombies with his bare hands for fun. Alphonse had picked Agent Seven personally, sending Hilda to get him out of prison and offering him fame, fortune, money and a chance to do whatever he wanted for three days without repercussion. Agent Seven had accepted and allowed himself to be handcuffed and a bag placed over his head while they transported him.

"Nothing happened to Agent Seven," Hilda replied. "He spent a long time standing in front of one of the cameras in City Two and made a list of demands for when this is all over. He said hello specifically to the people watching at home and gave a heart-warming speech about how thankful he is to the Controllers for giving him this chance."

"That sounds like a ratings boost right there."

"He's practically taken over City Two."

"There were six other people in City Two."

"Agent Seven took at least two of them hostage."

"Well, shit. Did we get this on camera?"

Hilda stiffened next to Alphonse. "Excuse me?"

"Do we have the hostages on camera?" Alphonse repeated. "Did I stutter?"

"I believe that Agent Seven was caught on camera abducting the other players at gunpoint as they woke up and started moving around City Two."

"Are they alive?"

Hilda hesitated. "For now, yes."

"Has he threatened to kill them?"

"Not as far as I'm aware."

Alphonse hummed and nodded to himself as he let his eyes wander back over the screens below him. "Well, I think that in light of all of this news, we will have to hold off on the zombies being released for a few more hours. Let's let our players sweat it out a bit longer. See if we can't shake things up in the morning."

Hilda nodded. "What instructions do you want me to give the staff?"

"None," Alphonse said, a slow, deranged smile creeping across his face. "I want radio silence. We're changing up the game. You can have them run the changes on-screen, but nothing is happening until the very early morning."

Hilda nodded and turned on her heel, a sick twisting nausea creeping up on her and making it difficult for her to hold her tongue. She walked away quickly and Alphonse made a note of the briskness in her step. He grinned to himself as he watched the workers in the Bullpen work frantically to try and fix the problems that Agent Seven and the destruction of City One had caused.

Ratings, Alphonse decided, were about to go through the roof.

CHAPTER SEVEN

Alphonse Ritter

"I hate zombies," Alphonse muttered, kicking in the rotting skull of a downed zombie as he stomped across the field. "Of all the things that human interference and mucking around with shit like chemical warfare and GMOs have brought around, this is the worst of all."

A dry chuckle answered Alphonse Ritter's complaints. He was in a company of five other armed men, his bodyguards, as he made his way through what was left of a neighbourhood housing complex he owned after an outbreak had spontaneously occurred. The complex had been a relatively large suburb made up mostly of rental properties. The townhouses across the street were also his, and the second semi-private community up the street was his as well. It was a six city block area made up of half-assed walled communities that were all for show and were rented out to yuppies who couldn't afford to buy a place, but wanted to feel like they were doing well for themselves. It was a scam and Ritter knew it. It was how he'd made a goodly chunk of his fortune. The difference between him and the faceless businesses who also owned properties like he did was that he actually cared and made sure that his tenants were as comfortable and well looked after as he could. He never said no to allowing people pets and he certainly made sure that things like plumbing were up to code. He wasn't a monster.

"Goddamn zombies," Alphonse muttered again as he surveyed the wreckage caused by idiocy and panic. "They're bad for business, you know."

"First responders did a fairly good job of keeping everything under control, you have to admit," one of the other men said.

Alphonse grunted. The man in question was named Jeremy Palmer. He was Alphonse's current right hand, a man skilled with numbers and keeping everything well organized. It was a bonus stroke of luck that Jeremy was just as happy with a gun in hand as he was behind a desk, and Alphonse was grateful to have him on his team.

"From the reports we got, there were fires set to try and neutralize the numbers of the infected. We were lucky that it was just the townhouses and not the single family homes that went up."

"And we're sure that it was arson?" Alphonse asked as he trudged back onto the paved roads that wound through the neighbourhood.

"Absolutely," Jeremy said with a nod. "It was started by a tenant who unfortunately didn't survive the outbreak."

"Damn shame," Alphonse replied. "I'd have liked to see what his insurance policy was."

Jeremy chuckled dryly.

"Looks like the outbreak has been neutralized at least," Alphonse continued as they made their way up to the first sopping wet townhouse. The fire department and the military responders had arrived on scene quickly and the outbreak was easily contained. Alphonse wasn't happy about it; spontaneous outbreaks were a death sentence for residential spaces. Where one occurred, another was believed to be more likely to happen, no matter what the original cause of the outbreak was. The problem with spontaneous outbreaks was that the original cause of the zombies was a virus that presented as a flu. It had started in college campuses and spread like wildfire when visiting prospects contracted the sniffles and went home. Every now and then, someone would contract the virus, spread it around the apartment building or school district, and a spontaneous outbreak would occur. When it happened to someone who wasn't elderly and the virus spread like wildfire, killing off tens or even hundreds of people in less than three days, the media was all over it. When it happened in a highly populated place, the media made it worse and protests would assuredly erupt, calling for stricter control of housing and medications.

"You could monetize on clean-up crews," Jeremy suggested as he and Alphonse stepped inside the first of the charred townhouses. "Run it in shifts, like firemen, put a crew in every neighbourhood you own and add a fee into the HOA and whatever fees. Up your rent a bit to subsidize the costs and to pay the responders you hire."

"You really think that would work?" Alphonse asked, stopping in the front entrance as Jeremy sidled up beside him to take in the damage.

"It would sure put a lot of people's minds at ease," Jeremy replied. "You could probably sell it to other contractors and have them pay you."

"You're deliciously evil," Alphonse said with a chuckle. "So what do you think about this?"

"Fire damage is worse than it looks in here," Jeremy said with a sigh as the two men walked further into the house. "We'd actually have to have building inspectors come in here after we gut the place to see if there are structural issues. If the fire damage on the others is worse than this, we're definitely remodelling."

Alphonse grunted. "This doesn't look like it was the start of the fire though."

"Likely not. The reports said that it started on the outer units and that there may have been a horde involved."

"God damn zombies," Alphonse muttered. "Like I said, there's no money to be made in them."

"I still think you can capitalize on frontline security to avoid situations like this."

"Duly noted," Alphonse agreed, sighing. "I'll look into it when we're done here. If the damage is worse in the other units, then let's write them all off. We'll see who is willing to move back in here. We'll release all the leases and return damage deposits. If people are willing to stay, they get their houses remodelled and we'll bulk up security in the back yards and stuff, all right?"

"Tax deductions will be great this year," Jeremy agreed. "As long as there's nothing major, the bulk of the remodels should be cosmetic. It sounds like the fire department got here before the flames could get too bad, which was lucky."

"Who neutralized the zombies?"

"Military first responders."

"Thank God for government funded gun-nuts."

Jeremy grunted. "We should go check upstairs to make sure that there's no major structural damage. Then we can start crunching numbers and making plans to fix these units."

"Good idea," Alphonse agreed. He led the way up the creaky stairs. The fire damage hadn't spread past the first two stairs and the men had no problem following them up to the second level.

The wallpaper was peeling in the hallway and water damage was evident on all of the walls. Alphonse swore under his breath as Jeremy poked at the ruined walls.

"At least they put out the fires?" Jeremy suggested as the drywall crumbled beneath his fingers.

"That was one hell of a lot of water," Alphonse complained. "Looks like it's going to be a gut job."

"Might as well upgrade them all," Jeremy offered. "Keep the rest the same, but remember that you're going to have empty units. The outbreak was larger than we've seen."

"Yeah yeah," Alphonse muttered. He stopped, holding up his hand with a frown of concentration on his face. "Did you hear that?"

Jeremy shook his head and moved his hand to his waist where his gun was holstered. Alphonse walked cautiously across the small mezzanine toward the master bedroom. He held his breath, his free hand dangling by his side, ready to draw his own gun, as he pushed open the door.

"Hello?"

A growl sounded from inside the room as the door opened with a squeak. Alphonse had no time to register what was happening as a tall, burly man leapt out from within the room and knocked him to the floor. The man was taller than Alphonse; well over six feet tall, and built like a linebacker. His eyes were wild, pupils dilated until the bright blue of his eyes was barely visible. His hair was wild and his teeth flashed like pearls in his gaping mouth. He was shirtless and dirty, hair matted to his head and looking like he'd been hosed down when the firemen had put out all the fires.

Alphonse grunted as he hit the floor and the wind was knocked out of him. The man on top of Alphonse howled and clawed at him, fingers digging into flesh and tearing fabric, but not drawing blood.

"Holy God, help me!" Alphonse croaked.

Jeremy was too slow on the draw and the man leaned forward to bite Alphonse's face. Alphonse's scream echoed through the house and alerted the men waiting outside Jeremy was on the man too late to keep him from damaging Alphonse, but he managed to pull him off of his employer before the damage could get too severe. Alphonse's screaming didn't stop as he stood up, still bleeding from the gaping wound on his face. Jeremy threw the attacker to the floor as Alphonse appeared, bleeding and screaming wordlessly beside him. They towered over the man and Alphonse spit blood.

Jeremy shuddered at the sight of his employer's ruined face.

Alphonse drew a ragged breath as he drew his gun. He didn't hesitate as he put two bullets into the man on the floor. The other men who had been meant to be acting as Alphonse's body guards stopped on the stairs, watching in horror as Alphonse stood, bleeding from the wound on his face and breathing heavily. Jeremy crouched down next to the dead man on the floor.

"Not a zombie," he announced. "Can't tell if he was infected."

"I'm fine," Alphonse snarled through his ruined face. "Get me to the hospital, and make sure that the rest of this neighbourhood is cleaned up before another incident occurs." He glared at the bodyguards. "Useless."

Jeremy jerked his head at the bodyguards, and then at the dead man on the floor as Alphonse shoved his way back down the stairs, dripping blood as he did. Jeremy followed, grinding his teeth and barely holding back the urge to vomit. The harsh sunlight only served to further the horror of Alphonse's injuries. Blood ran freely down his face and into the material of his expensive suit. Skin was torn and Alphonse's face was unrecognizable behind the mask of blood and tissue on the one side. The gouges from the homeless man's teeth had barely missed Alphonse's eye and Jeremy realized just how lucky Alphonse had actually been. Half a second and another quarter inch and he'd have been blinded. Jeremy shuddered and held back his retching, trying to think of something to say. Alphonse shook his head and reached into his pocket, pulling out a handkerchief. He shook it out, exposing the pristine white linen to the sun. He was moving stiffly, slowly, as if he was calculating every single motion as he did. Jeremy wondered if he was in shock. He opened his mouth to say something, but Alphonse beat him to it.

"I fucking hate zombies," Alphonse announced as he attempted to wipe the blood from his face with his handkerchief. "But I think that I just thought of a way to make them profitable for us."

CHAPTER EIGHT

Roll Call

The first night of the Rapture had gone off without any more surprises. The farmhouse stood a silent vigil over the barren landscape and Aya had made sure their fire hadn't gone out. The weather was holding, but it wasn't as warm as she'd expected. The house, at least, was comfortable and familiar. They had clear vantage points from inside, and would be able to see an oncoming horde if they kept an eye out. The large windows in the living room were Aya's only fear - the glass wasn't particularly thick and the zombies were persistent. Even with the plywood they'd put over them, it would only be a matter of time before anything broke its way through. Connor and Aya had warmed up some cans of food for dinner, sampling different flavours of soup and canned noodles, eating more than was strictly necessary, but they needed to do something to keep the panic from setting in, and there wasn't a shortage of rations in the house. Connor joked about anything that caught his attention, and he told Aya stories about when the apocalypse had first started, and how he'd been a saviour for the elderly in his neighbourhood. Aya listened intently, feeling safer with Connor's presence and more comfortable for having him around.

Bedtime was a point of contention. Connor wanted to sleep in the rooms, close themselves off from the rest of the world and try to pretend that this wasn't a kill or be killed situation. Aya argued with him, pointing out that they'd be sitting ducks if anything happened and they couldn't get out of the bedrooms.

"We're building a blanket fort and camping out in the living room."

Connor laughed it off and shook his head. "You're joking, right?"

Aya hadn't been kidding and she'd forced Connor to help her drag mattresses into the living room. They'd shared blankets and pillows and had made themselves as comfortable as they could given the circumstances. The fire had provided warmth and Aya had stoked it during her watch in the middle of the night, tossing more logs on to keep it going. It was a comfort to have it, the sounds of burning logs lulled Aya into a deeper sleep than she'd intended, though she didn't dream.

The crackle of mechanical static and the whine of a microphone being turned on too close to a speaker jolted Aya awake. She pushed herself up onto her elbows and glared at Connor. Her so-called partner had fallen asleep on his watch and had draped his arm over her while they slept. Aya shook Connor awake, cursing in Mandarin as she did.

"Sorry, I'm awake," Connor said as he sat up, wide-eyed, arm still draped over Aya's waist. "I was only resting my eyes."

"Yeah, sure," Aya sneered, shaking her head in disappointment as she removed Connor's arm from her lap. "You're just lucky there wasn't a horde let loose on us. Useless men," she added under her breath.

"Good morning players," the announcement droned. "Congratulations on surviving your first night in the Rapture. It's now six a.m., and we have plenty of surprises in store for you today."

"That's no good," Aya breathed.

"Surprises?" Connor asked.

"No, that's Alphonse Ritter's voice doing the announcements. He's the son of a bitch in charge of this who goddamn thing."

"So?" Connor asked, rubbing his eyes. "God, I'd kill for a coffee."

"So," Aya explained ignoring the fact that she would also kill for a coffee and they hadn't found any in the cupboards, "Alphonse Ritter doesn't usually get this involved. He's a figurehead, nothing more. He smiles for the camera and manages finances; he's not normally in the Controllers' headquarters. He's planning something."

"You've probably noticed the lack of the undead running around. You can thank the players left in City One for that, they managed to destroy two nests that we had waiting for you to take on. Well played gentlemen."

In the Bullpen, Alphonse leaned over the microphone, watching the monitors with glee as the views clicked between active cameras. The only monitor that hadn't changed was the one trained on Aya and Connor. That feed had been active most of the night, and rumours were already flying about the unlikely duo - and whether or not they'd become a couple. Aya Wu was a hot topic and the amount of money changing hands in bets on her survival was staggering. Alphonse was considering taking a bet and rigging the game to make it even more profitable for him. Maybe, he considered, he could retire once Aya was out of the way.

On the other hand, the rumour mill was running at full force, everyone was trying to figure out what exactly Aya Wu was planning, and how the strange Irishman was going to play into her plans. If she won, Aya would be one hell of a figurehead to flaunt as the winner until next time. The Internet and social media platforms were running wild with everything from "Save Aya" to "Ban the Rapture" and viewership was up by 30% overnight.

"I would also personally like to congratulate Miss Aya Wu on her selection for this year's Rapture. Miss Wu is a very big influence in this game, and while I don't normally get personal, or involved for that matter, I have decided that this was a special event and I thought it would be more appropriate for me to come here and personally oversee The Rapture because of Miss Wu's selection."

Aya stood up on the mattress, still fully clothed from the day before. "Hey, Alphonse," she crooned, looking directly at the camera above her. "I really hope this is broadcasting live."

"Just a moment, Miss Wu," the announcement said. Alphonse pushed a button and the live feed focussed solely on her, broadcasting across the world. "I have just switched the feed. You are being broadcast live to the whole world, and now is your chance to share a message with me, Alphonse Ritter, the Grand Controller of the Rapture, and the whole world."

Aya nodded slowly, a deranged grin spreading across her face. "Yeah," she said, loud enough to be sure that the camera would pick it up. "I've got one thing to say for sure."

Aya stood tall and stared the camera down. She raised both hands and flipped the bird directly into the camera and on live television. "Fuck this game, and fuck you, too. I'll see you soon, Alphonse."

Alphonse began to laugh, the cold, mirthless laugh of someone who was used to being threatened. His laughter echoed across the silent, empty fields and through the streets of Cities One and Two. The other players had no idea of why the Controller on the announcements was laughing, but it didn't sit well with anyone. Agent Seven shrugged and ignored it, getting back to building his own personal fortification, while the men in City One worked in stark silence to scavenge what they could.

In the Bullpen, Alphonse watched as the solidarity with Aya continued to grow, messages repeating "Fuck the Rapture" began cropping up and getting shared across all platforms. Alphonse needed to get things back under control.

"Well now," Alphonse crooned over the speakers, "I look forward to meeting the winners at the end of the three days. Back to business, though, we have had two hordes destroyed already, congratulations again to the players in City One. Since we are all a little miffed by this wrench in our otherwise smoothly running machine, you remaining players are getting a break and getting an additional four-hour reprieve from the shambling hordes. I would suggest that you use this time to scavenge up some extra ammunition, because as of now, you will no longer get warnings or map coordinates telling you where the hordes are being released from."

"What?" Connor shouted. "He's changing the rules! He can't do that!"

"He can do whatever he wants, Aya pointed out, turning away from the camera and dropping back down to sit on the mattress on the floor. "Now shut up and let the man talk."

Alphonse looked over at another monitor as pinging noises started sounding from a nearby computer. The outrage over the rules change was already hitting the internet and was already a trending topic worldwide, Aya's brief outburst seemed to have been forgotten by the crowds already, her outrage being replaced by confusion and speculation over the changes. He smiled to himself. Maybe Aya Wu wasn't going to be the biggest story of the Rapture this year, after all.

"So now you have four hours, and you get no more warnings from me. The announcements will be silent until tomorrow, unless I feel magnanimous and decide to give you all a fighting chance."

The click of the microphone being shut off echoed in the farmhouse.

Aya growled and threw a pillow and Connor sat with his head in his hands.

"Fuck," Connor muttered. "We're so fucked now, aren't we?"

"No more fucked than we were before," Aya replied with a shrug. She pulled herself up and stretched her arms over her head. "Except now we know that those explosions were intentionally set by the other players, and that there's been a major setback in the hordes. We're probably a lot safer here than we were yesterday, and there's a pretty good chance that the guys who are blowing up the town where you were dumped are in the same boat as us, and that they'll want to do whatever to get out of here, without killing anyone. It's not gonna do us any good to sit here and panic about anything, though. We haven't got enough information about anything yet, so let's just do what we're gonna do. Let's have breakfast," she suggested. "We should keep our strength up as best we can. There's still some vegetables from the garden, and some apples and berries from the trees. We can have hash browns and fruit compote. There's a bit of sugar in the pantry, it'll be a nice treat. Get your spirits up a bit, yeah?"

Connor groaned and laid back down, turning away from Aya. Aya crouched next to him and patted his shoulder. It was obvious that he was losing hope and the depression, caused by ending up in the Rapture when you were positive that you weren't going to make it, was creeping in on him. Aya didn't know how to help him; she wasn't trained to deal with the emotional implications of getting thrown into a forced survival situation. She knew that sugar would be helpful in keeping them from getting too depressed, and that food was a huge motivator. The people in the Rapture who ended up with the best rations were usually the ones who were better able to cope with the deteriorating circumstances. Making breakfast was one of the best things they could do, even if it wasn't as satisfying as bacon and eggs.

"Hey," she whispered, "we're gonna get out of here, I promise. I'm going to get you to your brother. It'll be okay."

"Yeah, all right."

"You don't believe me, do you?"

Connor sighed and rolled back over to look at Aya. Aya positioned herself between Connor and the camera on the wall and leaned forward, trying to keep the cameras and microphones that they were aware of from picking up their conversation as best they could. From behind her, she could hear the camera adjusting its angle, zooming in, presumably to try and pick up their conversation or to get a better view of whether they were making out or not.

"What makes you think that we're gonna survive this at all?" Connor asked.

"I'm not giving up, mostly," Aya replied, less confident than she sounded. "I'm going to shove my foot so far up the Rapture's ass that they won't be able to recover from this."

"And what if you die trying?"

Aya shrugged. "Then I get my name on a monument in a graveyard somewhere and someone else picks up the slack that will be left when I die. Especially if I die here. Do you think they these assholes are gonna win?"

"You can't really take them on from where you're sitting, Aya."

"No, but I can make their life a living hell."

"And you seriously think that sitting here, not participating, is gonna be the way to get them to shut up and listen to you?"

"No," Aya admitted. "But at least if I sit here and don't do a goddamn thing, they can't complain that I survived when no one else shoots me in the face."

"What do you think that Ritter guy is planning?"

"No idea. I've never met the guy. All I know is that he's the big boss of this whole operation and that he's got a hard on to get me out of the way."

Connor frowned. "Just because you protest his bullshit?"

Aya shrugged. "Doesn't matter. All that matters right now is that we're on the same page, right? We're partners now, stuck here, and we both have reasons to get outta this shit alive, right?"

"Yeah."

"So you're with me?" Aya pressed.

"I'm with you," Connor agreed.

"Good," Aya confirmed, nodding. "Remember, your brother's gonna be pissed off and doing anything he possibly can to get you back, right? You've gotta tough this one out for him. I'm inconsequential in the long run. There'll always be someone to replace me, and my mom and I got to say our goodbyes, but Mac? He's not gotten that chance yet, so let's not give the Controllers the satisfaction of taking that away."

"You think I'm suicidal?" Connor asked, a slow grin touching the corner of his lips. "Is that a touch of concern I detect, too?"

"I think you're depressed and dangerous," Aya corrected. "And that's not a good combination, especially since I've agreed to let you have weapons."

Connor clapped his hand over his chest. "I'm not suicidal. I promise."

Aya nodded. "We're gonna get out of here alive, okay?"

"Okay. Got a plan?"

Aya opened her mouth and looked up at the camera. She huffed a sigh, shook her head, and turned back to Connor. "Breakfast?"

CHAPTER NINE

City One

City One was a desolate place. It was small and sort of run down in that rural small town that didn't get many visitors sort of way that all prairie towns got eventually. There were normal conveniences, for the people who lived there, like gas stations, a small library, and a grocery store. There were several liquor stores and a bar, but nothing was exceptionally well cared for. Even the drug store felt like it had been abandoned for a long time. The houses were varied, relics of the times when they were built, mostly modernized, but never fully updated. There were concrete townhouses close to the sprawling brick schoolhouse, and a four-lane highway splitting the town in half.

The Controllers had intentionally dropped three players in City One. It was the larger of the two towns, and it housed the biggest hordes of zombies for the Rapture. City One, as it was called, was the farthest away from the town where the Controllers had set up their base. It wasn't difficult to set up a perimeter, though only Connor had seen the fence; the other players were too busy causing trouble.

The two men who remained in City One were polar opposites from one another, but they had decided to band together, rather than attempt the Rapture separately. They had spent a fitful night watching the flames lick at the buildings surrounding the explosions they'd caused, and keeping an eye out for other players, or more zombies. Sleep was a rare commodity for them, and the darker man had allowed his new friend to sleep most of the night, as the drugs to sedate them hadn't agreed with him.

"We fucked up."

The second man from City One chuckled. He was dark-haired, tanned skinned Slovak who had been living in North America since he was a child. He had gotten his citizenship at a young age and after his parents passed away, he joined the military, before being discharged for health reasons. He had, before being chosen to participate in the

Rapture, been doing charity work for people affected by the zombie outbreaks. He moved with the fluid grace of a martial artist, though he swore he wasn't particularly trained in anything more than shooting, running and killing. He smiled at his friend, the pale, skinny man who said he was an engineer but seemed to know his way around a knife and a crossbow better than he had any right to. The paler man was scarred on his arms and torso and while he was skinny, he was still more muscular than his new friend.

"Oh, don't talk like that, Topher," the darker of the two said. "We bought ourselves a good night's sleep, and you weren't in any shape to be running yesterday. I'm surprised you were able to come up with the bombs we used, and I'm happy that I was able to keep you from getting eaten."

Topher had reacted poorly to the drugs when he'd been dumped in City One. When Radek had found him, he was stumbling down the sidewalk, falling over himself and barely able to form a complete sentence. Radek had pulled him into a house and forced him to lie down on the couch until he was able to talk. When he did, the two formed a truce, neither wanted to participate, and considering how little luck Radek had had when it came to finding weapons or food, they agreed that it would increase their chances of survival exponentially to team up. They had agreed that staying in the house was a better idea and while Topher got sober, they devised a plan for building bombs and blowing up part of the city.

Topher shrugged and ran a hand through his blonde hair. "I don't know, I think we fucked ourselves. And I know you barely slept."

"We wiped out two nests. How is that, in any way, fucking ourselves? We've pretty much taken over the city. Not that it's very big, but still. And I'll be all right without sleep today; you were worse off than I was. Tonight though, you get to take a longer watch so I can rest. Or possibly, get a nap."

It had been Topher's knowledge of how to build an improvised explosive that had spurred the two on. Topher had suggested where they should look to place their weapons. They'd discovered two nests of sedated zombie hordes and taken them out. Radek had been impressed with the other man's performance, even suffering major withdrawal symptoms, and being shaky, Topher had figured out the most logical places where the Controllers would have stored their weaponized zombies.

The open doors in the alleys and broken, full-length glass windows had been a major tip-off, too. Even with the decoy buildings set to look like they housed hordes, Topher had managed to figure out where the actual hordes were being stored with only one false start. Radek had placed the bombs and set the detonators while Topher waited a good distance away. He'd been willing to take that risk to help his new companion while he fully recovered from his sedation.

Topher snorted. "Radek, you're much too good of a person for this."

Radek laughed. "And you're still hiding secrets from me, my friend."

Topher shrugged again, it was becoming his go-to reply for anything that he wasn't quite comfortable with. And there was a lot of stuff he wasn't quite comfortable with in the Rapture. "Secrets are part of the game, right? You don't need to know everything about me, and I won't ask after you. All you need to do is trust that I'm not gonna kill you in your sleep."

"Well, I trust that," Radek promised.

Topher nodded again and sighed. "I still think we fucked up. They're changing the rules on us? That's unheard of."

"Yeah, but so is throwing one of the biggest pains in the ass of the entire Rapture system in the mix for this year's event."

"You mean that Aya person?"

"Please," Radek sneered, his accent thickening in his agitation. "As if you don't know who Aya Wu is?"

Topher held up his hands in a no contest sort of gesture. "I know who she is. I've never had the pleasure of meeting her before though."

"Neither have I."

"Depending on how the rest of this goes down, you might not get that chance."

"I hope that she's in less danger than we were," Radek admitted.

"I'm sure she can handle herself."

"Do you agree with her? About the exploitation involved with this whole game show?"

Topher shrugged. "Hard to say. I mean, we're in the middle of this damned game aren't we? Saying that yes, I think she's right is a bit self-serving of me at this point."

Radek chuckled. "All right, so we've got a few gallons of gas left, a working vehicle, and a handful of ammo. How's the food situation?"

"We've got some bottled water, some Gatorade that's on the cusp of expiration, some gum, a couple chocolate bars and two small bags of beef jerky."

"Shit."

"We've been all over this town, and there's been like what? A tiny ass cache of weapons that wouldn't have been enough to hold off those hordes if they woke up, and a bag of chips. We had a can of spaghetti between us yesterday and those potato chips for supper. They don't want us getting out of here."

"I think they do want us to get out of here. I think that they wanted to drive us out of this town, Topher," Radek said. "That's why the hordes were so big, and that's why there's no food or ammunition. They want us to keep going."

"Why?"

Radek shrugged. "I think that they expected us to kill each other."

"I appreciate you not shooting me."

"I wonder where that other guy we saw got to?"

Topher shrugged. "I wish he'd have stayed, at least we'd have an extra guy to keep watch."

"I hope he didn't get eaten," Radek agreed.

"Considering that none of the hordes were out of their stasis yet?" Topher asked. "I think it's highly unlikely that he was eaten. I hope he's holed up somewhere, maybe if he's still in town we can join forces."

"That would be good," Radek agreed.

"You know what? I really don't wanna stay here."

"All right, let's pack up the truck. I don't know what else to do. We should drive, I guess, see what else we can find? Maybe we can find some food, and worst case we can drive into the fields away from buildings to try and keep far enough away from the zombies that we don't have to worry as much? There's farmland around here, right? I think we could reasonably lay low out there. Steal a farmhouse to hole up in? Maybe find some other players?"

Topher made a non-committal noise and bobbed his head before answering. "It's up to you, man. You're the brains of this operation. I just know how to shoot a crossbow and build IEDs."

Radek laughed and offered Topher a hand to help him up. "Okay, let's pack up, do one more search to try and find something to eat, and maybe a few more weapons, and then get the hell out of here."

Topher accepted Radek's hand and let the other man pull him to his feet. He was still exhausted, feeling worn out from the drugs and the adrenalin rush of blowing up half a city with no police repercussions. It wasn't something that Topher particularly wanted to get used to, but it was serving him well, so far. He nodded, resolutely, to Radek as his stomach growled and he grinned sheepishly at the gurgle.

"I think you're right, and we ought to look for food first. We're not gonna get too far if there's nothing in our bellies."

Radek chuckled and clapped his new friend on the shoulder. "Thank you for joining my team."

"I wouldn't call it a team..."

"Then thank you for being my friend in all of this."

Toper felt a sick knot settle itself in the pit of his stomach at the thought of being Radek's friend. He knew that this wasn't the kind of situation that was conducive to making friends, and he wondered how far Radek would go to protect that friendship, and alternatively, how far Radek would go if he was pushed. He wondered if Radek was the kind of man to shoot someone he called his friend if push came to shove, or if he was the kind of person to lay down his life for a so-called friend.

"You're still far too kind of a person to be here," Topher said after a long moment "You're lucky to have me on your side."

Radek laughed as he led the way out of the house and into the cool morning air. Radek paused outside the house, staring up at the two storey building, wondering where the family who had lived there went, and whether they were going to return tot he city after the Rapture was over for the year. Topher caught up to him in barely a moment, giving him a gentle shove as he passed.

"Come on, Radek, there's no time to get sentimental about a place that isn't yours."

Radek sighed and nodded. He knew that Topher was right. It was pointless to worry about the people who were gone; they were compensated and were allowed to return back to their homes, if they wanted to, although to be honest, Radek had never spoken to anyone who had ever returned to their home after a Rapture Program had happened in their city. It was dismal and emotionally draining to see the houses left almost completely intact, with unimportant items still in the cupboards and on the walls. At least, Radek considered, there hadn't been any personal photos left on the walls to further drive home the fact that there had been people living there before the Rapture.

"You're taking too long!" Topher shouted from the truck they'd hot-wired. He had climbed into the passenger seat and was dangling out of the car, lazily swinging his arms and legs like a kid who needed to go to the bathroom on a long car ride. "If you don't hurry up and forget about this ridiculous nostalgia thing you've got going on, romanticizing the fact that we're in someone else's house and they might never come back, then I'm gonna leave without you. And I'm taking the supplies you so graciously left in the truck."

Radek grinned, flashing his teeth and giving Topher the middle finger as he did as he was told, forgetting, albeit momentarily, that they were in the middle of a deadly game show where they weren't guaranteed to wake up the next day. He hurried around to the driver's side of the truck and climbed in. He buckled himself in and Topher slammed his own door.

"Where to?" Radek asked.

"I think we should go check out this town a little more, what do you think?"

"There's drugstore around here, right?" Radek asked.

"Yeah, I think I saw one on Main Street?"

"Is that the street we're calling Main Street?" Radek teased as he started the car.

"Sure why not?" Topher asked, leaning back in his seat as his stomach growled again. "I think there's a pizza place around here somewhere, too. Can we check it out?"

"Lead the way, if you think you can remember where it is through the fog of that bad reaction you had."

"Yeah," Topher mumbled. "I think I remember where I saw it. Not like there's a huge area for us to look for it if I'm wrong," he added.

Radek laughed again and eased the truck away from the driveway, humming to himself as he did. Topher stared balefully out the window, wondering vaguely if they would actually be able to make it through to the end. He couldn't let himself ride high on the victory of destroying two hordes, there was more to the Rapture than that, and they had made themselves *very* known to the people in charge. If there wasn't a retaliation against them by the Controllers, Topher would be surprised. Obviously, they could change the rules on the fly; it wouldn't surprise him in the least if they could throw something in their way that wasn't supposed to have been there. He sighed and closed his eyes, hoping that Radek was as helpful and kind as he seemed to be so far.

Radek turned carefully onto the Main Street, away from the highway that would lead out of the city, still humming to himself, and keeping his eyes open for the pizza joint Topher said he saw. He was hungry, too, and he hoped that there would be even a tin of pineapple; it would be enough to hold him over for the next day, if they made it. He stole a glance at Topher, who still had his eyes closed, and he couldn't help but wonder how he could be so calm and distant in the face of such an atrocity. Radek had been in the military, but it hadn't suited him, he'd managed to keep his humanity intact. Topher, on the other hand, seemed like he'd been through the Rapture, at least, once before and Radek hoped that he would warm up to him, eventually.

"Hey look," Radek announced as he slowed the car. "You were right. You want a pizza?"

CHAPTER TEN

Radek

The military really didn't suit Radek, and he'd known it even before he joined up. He wasn't sure what had possessed him to join. He thought it was desperation, and fear of being useless, but it didn't sit right with him. His parents had been the ones to suggest military life to him when he was in high school. He was highly intelligent and he got bored so easily, they thought the strict rigidity of life in the military would be good for him. Radek had avoided joining the military after high school, and when his parents died in a plane crash on the way home from visiting the Old Country, he decided to honour them by doing what they had wished of him before their deaths.

Military life was not something that Radek was well suited for. He was quiet and bookish, and while he was in good physical shape overall, he wasn't prepared for the training that went into becoming a military man. It was gruelling, boot camp nearly killed him, and yet he pushed on to get through. He managed to get himself discharged for medical reasons before the apocalypse hit, and he refused to enter back into service when zombies started showing up.

Radek lived in a rural area, in the home that his parents had bought before they died. It wasn't farmland, but it was far enough out of the city to make a midnight fast food run a pain in the ass. He had two acres all to himself, with thick rows of trees around the edge of the property, and a low retaining wall stretching around the entire two acres. It was his own little slice of heaven in the middle of the apocalypse. The house was too big for him and most of it went unused. He didn't mind. It meant that he could entertain people easily, but he never did. He wasn't particularly social.

Radek worked online, doing data entry and taking customer calls whenever they came in. It wasn't glamorous, but it kept the bills paid. He had a garden and fruit trees and maintained them during the apocalypse, spending his evenings tending to his plants and making preserves. It was a quiet life and it worked for him, kept him out of trouble.

Trouble was Radek's middle name and his parents had known it. Radek was doing his best to avoid trouble, but trouble tended to seek him out, take him by the hand and show him the time of his life, even when he wasn't looking. He had spent a lot of his teenage years actively rebelling against anything that caught his attention. Society in general needed a good, hard reboot, and he found himself running with anarchists of all kinds. He'd learned to make IEDs, how to shoot, how to encrypt digital files, and how to get around most encryptions. He was incredibly smart and he picked up on things quicker than most people, and then perfected his techniques. By the time he had forged medical documents to get out of the military, he knew he needed to back off from the things that he was doing before he got into real trouble. He retreated back to his family home and took on boring jobs that wouldn't get him in trouble. He spent his downtime tending to his garden and keeping a generally low profile.

When the first Rapture happened, Radek was in his mid-twenties and he watched online with the rest of the world. He was shocked and angry by the brazen display of callous lack of humanity put forth by the contestants. A three-day pass to murder in exchange for money. No rules, except survive. It was worse than the gladiators of Rome.

And humanity was lapping it up.

The second year of the Rapture brought in corporate sponsors and a cable television slot. It was suddenly more important than any professional sporting event and was more popular than the Olympics and the Oscars combined. Radek sat slack-jawed, watching the event unfold on television just like everyone else in the world. Radek, however, eventually sought out the online communities that covered the Rapture. He was looking for information about the event. Who ran it? Where did they get their money? How did the government actually allow this to happen? Was it because year one had been death row inmates? Year two had introduced the lottery. Supposedly all citizens, no matter where they lived, were entered into the random drawing to participate in the Rapture. There was no getting out of it, it was worse than a forced conscription.

Every other year, the Rapture happened, pitting ten randomly selected contestants against each other in a demilitarized zone or abandoned city, and unleashing hordes of zombies. Every other year, the world sat in unbridled fascination as they watched the 'game' unfold on their televisions. Every other year, the people rallying against the Rapture would come out of the woodwork, filling forums and social media, loudly protesting online. And then they'd disappear.

The longer that Radek dug, the worse the rumours about the Rapture got. There were supposed systems in place to randomly select the contestants, but the darker online communities suggested that this wasn't the case. The world was blind and ignorant, according to some forums, willing to believe whatever lie the propaganda machine would churn out and spoon-feed to the masses, but these online bell ringers knew the truth. They claimed that the Rapture's lottery was rigged, that Big Brother was watching and the players weren't so 'randomly' selected as they were specifically chosen for their skills, abilities, and past behaviours. They claimed that Big Brother was watching everyone like a hawk, worse than they ever had before, except this time it wasn't for government protection against supposed terrorists, it was for people who would make for the best contestants in the Rapture. They claimed that the world was watching and Big Brother was watching the world. They would pluck people from the streets in broad daylight if they exhibited consistent behaviours that would make for excellent television. Rarely did they see preppers or survival experts taking part in the Rapture. Usually it was frat boys, and mild mannered schoolteachers, and people verging on psychosis on the best day of the week pitted against each other, the complete cultural imbalance, the yin and yang of society as it were. It was meant to be a cutthroat event, where killing was not only allowed, but typically necessary to ensure your own survival. The less stable you were, the less you clung to the rules of society and general good behaviour, the more likely you were to be able to survive the three days.

The first Rapture events ended in massive bloodshed with no clear winner. No one survived and it was usually because the last one or two people had killed the rest of the contestants and weren't able to hold off the massive hordes that were unleashed by the end of the game. The outcry that it was rigged to be in favour of the Corporation running the event sounded loud and clear once prisoners weren't the only people playing the game. The families of the contestants were never available to be reached for public comment. The Internet said that they were paid off to remain silent. The Corporation, of course, denied all of the rumours and made a show of having people whose loved ones had been contestants in the Rapture come on camera and give a statement. No one really said anything of any importance. They read canned statements, talking about the true honour of having their family members or loved ones randomly selected for the Rapture. They always mentioned how proud they were and how obviously sad they were that their loved ones hadn't made it, but that's not their fault because they weren't made for survival. Press questions were never allowed, and society just accepted it as part of the mourning process. None of the players' families ever appeared to have any more money than they had before the Rapture, so the hush money theory soon disappeared and families of the contestants became talk show circuit celebrities. No need for hush money when they were paid for public appearances to talk about how they were handling the effects of the Rapture.

The third Rapture, however, things changed. People got more organized and the protests that had been regulated to tabloid fodder, or otherwise completely hushed up, exploded. People were livid and made damn sure that the Corporation knew it. Radek watched the protests unfold on television in the weeks leading up to the Rapture with a morbid fascination. These were the people most vehemently opposed to the Rapture, These were survivors of the apocalypse, and the ones who still considered themselves humanitarians. These were the people who knew what it was like to have everything taken away from you, and what it was like to have to shoot someone you had once loved in the head because of the infection that killed them and made them into a flesh-eating monster.

Radek watched as a young woman appeared on his television. She was dirty, covered in dried mud and dirt from the protests, with scrapes on her hands. She was dressed in jeans and a military-style jacket and was comforting a crying older woman and Radek found himself drawn to the spectacle on TV.

"This is Katie Fitzgerald," the girl shouted at the gathered reporters. "Her son was a contestant in the last Rapture. She has been in hiding since then, unable to speak, unable to do a damn thing. She has been bullied and intimidated into silence."

"I didn't take any of the money they offered me," Katie sobbed. "They showed up at my house, offering cold condolences and a lot of money to buy my silence. I didn't take it. I told them to go to hell and I've been running ever since. Now, I'm not afraid of them. My son died in the Rapture. He called me when he found out about where he was. He was scared, he was crying. He begged me to get him home before his phone was cut off. They jam the signal. I wasn't able to call him back. I wasn't able to say goodbye..."

Katie broke back down into sobs that shook her whole body. The entire crowd of reporters fell into shocked silence. No one dared to say anything and break the reverence of Katie sobbing into her hands with the young girl patting her back.

The girl was the one to break the silence.

"My name is Aya Wu. I'm sure you all know who I am by now, and if you don't, then Google me. I've seen firsthand the hell that comes out of the Rapture. I've been in the places left over after the show is done. I've been on the clean-up crews who try and make the game arenas liveable again. The Rapture is a piece of filth, it is a cancer on our society and it's high time that we come together and raise our voices and have it stopped."

The crowd leapt into a feeding frenzy of journalism. Aya didn't flinch as she was bombarded with questions shouted at her. She answered calmly, but with the weight of emotion and exhausting and rage behind her words. She had her people to support her and she spoke with clarity, never swearing and never being bitter for rhetoric. She had the practised manner of someone well groomed to speak in the public eye, although Radek had never seen her or even heard of her before this impromptu press conference. She was wild and angry and beautiful. Her passion was a fire that would ignite a thousand torches. She was Helen of Troy, ready to start the war against the Rapture.

Radek jumped into action. He was on his computer searching up ways to unblock jammed phone signals. He was on his forums, talking with other people, looking for more information on the girl on his television. He knew that he needed to do something about the Rapture. Even if he was just another body in the line of pepper spray and tear gas when it boiled down to the protests, he just couldn't sit idly by and not move.

By the Fourth Rapture, Radek was on the front lines. He was known for helping people who were gassed. He was a medic without training, but learned from experience. He had emergency kits and gave them out whenever he was around, and he wasn't shy about getting in the way of rubber bullets if it meant that someone else didn't need to experience it.

He never caused property damage directly, but he guided the angrier people from the sidelines, explaining ways to do the most damage with the least amount of effort. He watched with unbridled glee as his words were used to make statements. Property damage against the Corporation and against the Rapture soared and there was nothing to tie him specifically back to it. He couldn't help but feel a pang of pride every time the protests he wasn't involved in took a violent turn. Sometimes, the only way to make sure that your voice was heard was to light a car on fire and shout from the rooftops. He did, however, always instruct his people to ensure that no one who wasn't involved got hurt. They weren't killers, and there was no point in harming anyone to prove a point. That would make them no better than the

Corporation and would undermine their cause. He was a force to be reckoned with, a force for good among the ranks of the protestors, and even more vocal about organizing things on the Internet backend.

Maybe, he decided, his parent had been right.

When they came for him, they did it quietly. They didn't Taser him in the mall parking lot. They didn't pull him out of the protesting crowd and throw him in the back of a waiting police van and have him disappeared. They showed up at his house.

Radek answered the door when the bell rang. He wasn't expecting anyone; no one ever came to visit him. Standing on his porch was a man with a scarred and mutilated face, a tall blonde woman who looked like she could kill Radek if he sneezed the wrong way, and a stouter man in military clothes.

Radek smiled. "Come on, in. Kettle is on, I'll bring out some refreshments. Have a cup of a tea, I promise I'm not the kind of person to poison you. I've been waiting for you guys to show up, kind of expecting you to. I'll come quietly, no need to cause a scene."

"You think we're taking you somewhere?" the scarred man asked.

"Please," Radek said, his accent slipping and making the word a husky drawl. "You're Alphonse Ritter. You're either here to kill me for my involvement in the protests against the Rapture, or I've been lucky enough to have been chosen to participate this year. Either way, come in, have a cup of tea and something to eat, and let's talk for a few minutes, then I'll accept whichever fate you've decided is appropriate for me without a fuss."

Alphonse Ritter smiled as Radek held the door open and stepped aside, welcoming his enemy into his home. The kettle whistled from the kitchen and Radek showed his guests into the living room while he went to make the tea.

Alphonse looked at Hilda and smiled again. "Now if only everyone was this agreeable to coming and playing our game, we would have a much easier time of it, wouldn't we?"

Hilda nodded but said nothing.

In the kitchen, Radek could hear every word, and he breathed a heavy sigh. It was a death sentence either way, but at least he could make an attempt from inside. Maybe this would be the last year of the Rapture, after all.

CHAPTER ELEVEN

Hostage Situation

Agent Seven dragged one of his hostages outside, shoving the confused woman to where the others had already been lined up. He had rounded up five hostages, and he was thrilled to have them at all. It was his bargaining chip, his sacrifice to the zombies, and he'd have no problem leaving them behind. He had spent the night building a barricade out of old barbed wire, and cars. He had rigged up empty cans and bottles in a string maze to warn him of anyone approaching on the main road. Agent Seven had chosen a house as his headquarters just off the main road, behind the church. City Two was less than half the size of City One, little more than a collection of tiny houses and modified trailers set up long a main road and stretching out around the single stretch of highway at the bottom of a valley.

They had told Agent Seven everything about the game They had explained the rules to him, and how anything that he did within the confines of the three days of the game would not be held against him. They told him that he was a prime candidate to participate, and if he won, he'd have more money than he'd know what to do with. The allure of fame and fortune didn't interest Agent Seven as much as the idea that he could do whatever he wanted for three days did. Money and fame was nice, as long as he survived. Part of him didn't trust the people who were throwing him, blindfolded, into the back of a van to be dropped off and left for dead in a town he'd never been to. He wasn't entirely sure that he'd be allowed to walk away after the game was over, but he didn't really care. He had found five hostages in the game. They would be his bargaining chips to make sure he got out of the Rapture alive, and to make sure that no one else backed out of the deal. He'd made a list of demands to the indifferent CCTV camera, but he wasn't sure if anyone heard him. No one had addressed him during the morning announcements, no one had reached out since, and he was starting to wonder if the Controllers had double-crossed him.

No matter, Agent Seven decided. He had five hostages, and a base filled with booby traps.

He had food, and weapons and he was sure that he could hold off the Controllers if they decided that he wasn't allowed to escape justice for any crimes he may or may not commit in the span of the three days of the Rapture. He dragged his final hostage from the house and forced her to walk down the street to where the others had been tied. They were spaced twenty feet apart and were on the very edge of the booby traps he'd set up to trap zombies, or other players as the case might be. His hostages were bait, and if the Controllers did what he wanted, he would consider releasing them.

The woman was a tall, black woman dressed in skinny jeans and a leather jacket. She had a fire in her eyes and she was limping. Agent Seven had ambushed her and tried to hobble her with a bat. She'd fought him off, mostly, but the injury to her leg had proven to be too much at the time and he overpowered her. She glared at the surroundings, not particularly pleased to be a part of the Rapture, and even more angry about the fact that she'd been kidnapped by a psychopath.

Agent Seven shoved her and she stumbled, catching herself before her injured leg gave out completely. He sighed and rolled his eyes, giving the woman a sour look as she instinctively curled up to favour her injured leg. Agent Seven couldn't tell if she was crying or not, and he didn't much care either way. He let her whine and hold herself for a moment before he finally spoke.

"Get a move on," Agent Seven sneered.

"Or what?" the woman asked. "You'll kill me?"

"Pretty much."

"Seems like you're gonna do that either way."

"You can die here, or you die later," Agent Seven offered. "If you're lucky, the Controllers will do what I ask and you'll get to try your hand at surviving the game on your own."

"And if I'm not lucky?"

Agent Seven made a choking noise as he drew his finger across his throat.

The woman rolled her eyes as she forced herself to stand up. Agent Seven didn't help her. It took two false starts for her to roll over enough to get her injured leg under her and bearing enough weight to carry her, and as soon as she was up, Agent Seven shoved her again. "Get moving."

"I don't think so," she said.

"I said, move it," Agent Seven snarled, reaching out to shove her again.

Agent Seven didn't see it coming. He hadn't expected her to fight anymore, not after the baseball bat incident. She turned and struck Agent Seven with a sharp jab of her fingers to his throat. Agent Seven's eyes bulged and he dropped the gun he was holding as he grabbed at his throat. The woman swung a punch, catching Agent Seven in the side of the face and sending him sprawling to the ground. She grabbed the gun he'd dropped and took off running as fast as he wounded leg would allow her. Agent Seven drew the pistol he wore at his hip and took aim at the woman. He hesitated pulling the trigger and then thought better of it. Gunshots tended to attract both the living and the dead, and he wasn't about to get caught with his proverbial pants down just so he could have the satisfaction of shooting the limping woman.

He watched as she limped her way away, disappearing as she took a corner and made her way between the houses. There would be time to deal with her later. She only had a few rounds in the gun she'd stolen from him, and there were no more announcements about the zombies. He wasn't happy to have lost a hostage. They were the only thing keeping him alive and well employed for the duration of the game.

Tucking his gun away, he watched her run on her injured leg. Obviously, he hadn't broken it, but he'd done a good enough job to slow her down. Between the other players that Agent Seven hadn't rounded up as hostages, and the zombies, he wasn't too worried about losing her. She was injured and armed with a gun she didn't know how to use. She wouldn't last. Agent Seven snarled and spit blood on the ground. If she came back, he would deal with her when the time came. No sense worrying over her for the time being. He still had work to do.

CHAPTER TWELVE

Agent Seven

The screams of his victims still haunted his dreams. No one wanted to get anywhere near him, even in prison. He slept soundly; safe in the knowledge that he'd done everything he possibly could to make sure that everyone else thought he was crazy.

Maybe, he decided, he was crazy.

That would have explained a lot about him.

He hadn't always been called Agent Seven, that was a name given to him by the Controllers when he was picked up for The Rapture. He'd been called a lot of other things over the course of his gory career, though. The Fairway Killer had been his favourite title.

He was just a guy, doing his work, so what if society thought it was wrong to kill women in back alleys? He wasn't discriminating against anyone. As far as he was concerned, the women he was killing were meant to die, why else would they have been put in his path? Everything, he reminded himself as they had slapped the handcuffs on him, happened for a reason.

He had always managed to stay one step ahead of the police investigating his crimes and he'd managed to slip through the cracks of the judicial system more times than seemed humanly possible. He knew his luck would run out, eventually, and when they picked him up in one of the squatters' warehouses where he had been mercilessly beating zombies to death with his bare hands, and threw him in the maximum-security prison to evaluate him, he had thought that his luck had finally run out.

The prison was barely warmer than the warehouse, and the wind whistled through the cracks in the concrete. The prisons had been used as initial safe houses when the dead began to rise. People had filled the spaces where the prisoners had been moved out of. The upper levels were where they'd put the criminals, piling them five-deep in the small cells, forcing the inmates to sleep on whatever flat surface they could find. Exercise was non-existent for the prisoners in the first few days of the apocalypse. Cabin fever mingled with the smell of sweat and fear and inmates did more damage to each other than the zombies had been doing outside.

The common areas were turned into civilian sleeping areas and the smell of unwashed human bodies filled the concrete structures even more than usual. Spontaneous outbreaks had occurred in the first days of the apocalypse. People crammed that many upon each other were prone to getting sick. The fever ripped through them and before anyone could react, there were outbreaks and zombies eating people. Eventually, they had no choice but to arm the prisoners to protect the people and kill the zombies. It worked well, until the prisoners had turned against the police and military, and started rioting.

The prisons were never entirely fixed and the wind whistled through the cracks like screaming women.

Agent Seven took more comfort from the howling wind than anyone else. It lulled him to sleep, and forced everyone else to rethink messing with him.

The prison guards ran his prints and facial recognition and left him alone. Agent Seven killed his first man at dinner on his third night in jail. The bigger inmate had tried to assert his dominance, stealing Agent Seven's food and pushing him out of his seat. Agent Seven hadn't taken kindly to the interruption and he jumped on the man's back, screaming bloody murder as he ripped his jugular out with his teeth. He howled as the inmate dropped to the ground, convulsing as the blood pumped out of the gaping wound and Agent Seven climbed up onto the table, triumphant. His eyes were black pits as he stared at the other prisoners, blood running from his mouth and all down the front of his orange jumpsuit.

"Anyone else want to try?" he crooned. No one answered, the shocks and horror that washed over the remaining inmates was palpable. Agent Seven smirked as he stood on top of the table. He waited for a long moment to make sure that no one else was going to try anything, before jumping down and sauntering across the room to retrieve another plate of prison food. The server didn't say anything when Agent Seven asked for a larger helping and an extra glass of water, he just gave him what he requested. Agent Seven crossed the room back to where he had been sitting, stepping lightly over the fresh corpse of his attacker, ignoring the puddle of blood he had to step in to get back to his seat, and sat back down. He took a bite of lunch, chewing thoughtfully, then shrugged and continued his meal.

No one else dared to harass him after that. Even the guards weren't sure what to make of him. First the zombies with his bare hands, then the inmate with his teeth. There was nothing that would strike fear into him, and the guards could see it in his eyes.

Solitary confinement as a punishment only meant that he could sleep undisturbed. The howling winds were worse there, and Agent Seven spent most of his time lulled to sleep in the week in solitary by the screams of his victims riding the winds.

When the transfer came, Agent Seven felt the first real pangs of fear clench his guts and make his blood run cold. They came for him in the middle of the night, dragging him out of solitary and roughly walking him. He fought at first, the disorientation from being woken so suddenly triggering his fight or flight mode. When his brain woke up enough to register what the guards were screaming at him, however, he stopped kicking and gnashing his teeth. Transfers weren't a bad thing, were they? He didn't know, he'd never been in the system.

They shoved a bulletproof vest over his head and strapped it against his chest before shoving a helmet on his head. The helmet was too big and partially obscured his vision and his head rattled around inside it as the guards hustled him out of the solitary cell and down the hallway. Agent Seven was half dragged, his bare feet slipping against the cold floor whenever he couldn't get enough purchase to walk himself. Eventually, he gave up and allowed the guards to drag him along, lifting him down the stairs as they took him to the waiting van outside.

The rush of fresh air as they made their way outside ripped across his skin and rustled the thin fabric of his prison jumpsuit. They hadn't let him keep the bloodstained one and he lamented it. They came to a stop outside, before they got into the waiting vans, and the helmet was removed from Agent Seven's head. He blinked in the harsh daylight, squinting against the sun. Standing in front of him, there was a severe looking woman, with her hair tied back in a bun. Agent Seven's heart raced in his chest at the sight of her. He hadn't seen another woman this close since the apocalypse had happened - at least, not a real woman. He'd been preoccupied with the undead and he'd let his true calling pass him by temporarily.

"Pick your jaw up off the floor," the woman snapped, her words clipped and coloured by a sharp German accent. "I am perfectly aware of who you are and what you do. It has been my employer who has kept the records of your crimes concealed from the police for as long as they have been. You're not as lucky as you think."

Agent Seven tilted his head and licked his lips. Her words had struck a chord and his heart rate spiked again as his stomach dropped. They'd known? His records alone would have sent him to the chair three times over, and considering how many times he'd been picked up and held for a few days while they tried to identify him, and place him as one of the various serial killers that had been terrorizing the various cities he found himself in, he thought he'd just been careful.

"You do understand the gravity of this situation that you find yourself in yes?" the woman asked.

Agent Seven nodded.

"You have a very extensive record of violence, you should be executed, but my employer has been watching your career for the last several years. He has bought your records and had them temporarily expunged. If you agree to our terms, your records will stay vanished and you will get to walk free. If you work for us, and do as you're told, you will get a large sum of money which I cannot and will not discuss here, as well as a fresh start set up somewhere that I also cannot disclose while we have ears around that do not belong to our payroll. You will not be asked to do anything that you're otherwise normally uncomfortable with, and the rewards for following our orders will be incrementally greater based on your performance."

Agent Seven smiled coolly and ran his tongue across his teeth. He knew this woman wasn't meant for him, and he would be remiss to try and fight his way out of this confrontation. "And what happens if I say no?"

The woman shrugged. "If you say no, then I make a phone call. Your records reappear and you get whatever the judicial system thinks is an appropriate punishment for your crimes. From what I understand, there are more than a few prisoners and guards here who would like nothing ore than to beat you senseless. I also understand that the brutal crimes you've committed against mostly women are cause for nasty retribution like beatings and starvation torture. Things that normally get swept under the rug in light of zombie attacks and spontaneous outbreaks within a prison."

"And you're going to orchestrate all of this, I suppose?"

"Whatever happens to you if you say no thank you to our most generous offer isn't my concern," the woman replied with a nonchalant shrug. "My employer and I only care about your answer. Yes, or no."

Agent Seven peered around the prison yard. The wind never stopped blowing, and it was cold. He didn't particularly want to take his chances back inside the joint, but he also didn't entirely trust the woman standing in front of him with her vague promises and her clipped speech.

"Time is wasting," she said after a moment. "You need to make up your mind because this is a time sensitive offer."

"Okay," he said with a nod. "Anything you want, get me the hell out of here."

The woman smiled and snapped her fingers. Agent Seven was shoved forward, roughly and two new guards appeared from the sides of the van. They grabbed him again and shoved a rough black bag over his head. They lifted him from the ground, carrying him to a different van than the one they'd been standing in front of, one that Agent Seven hadn't noticed. They spoke in rapid German, words that sounded harsh and that Agent Seven couldn't understand. He felt the cold clasp of handcuffs clamp around his arms as he was ushered into the inside of another van. His legs were similarly shackled and chained to a point inside the vehicle so he couldn't fight his way out. The rumble of the engine sounded and the doors slammed shut.

"I'm glad you said yes," another voice crooned above all the German. "I didn't think that a man as accomplished as you would be stupid enough to say no to my offer."

"Don't answer," the German woman snapped. "Just listen."

Agent Seven nodded his head, bobbing the bag instead.

"My name is Alphonse Ritter," the man continued. "Congratulations, you've been randomly selected for this year's Rapture. Do you understand what that is?"

The Rapture. He definitely knew what that was. And he was definitely excited to be a part of it. He nodded.

"Excellent," Alphonse said. "I believe that my lovely assistant Hilda has told you that we are offering you a fresh start, so long as you do as we say, yes?"

He nodded under the bag again.

"Good, I'm glad that we are all on the same page. May I tell you what we want you to do?"

CHAPTER THIRTEEN

Minor Setback

"Thank you for breakfast," Connor said.

"Wash the dishes," Aya replied with a smirk as she got up from her spot on the floor. "And please don't let the fire go out."

"Are you planning on going somewhere?"

"Yeah," Aya agreed with a nod. "I'm going to go see if there's anything useful in the houses down the road."

"You can't leave!"

Aya arched her eyebrow and stared at Connor. "I can't?"

"Not by yourself!"

"Look," Aya explained, placing her hands on her hips. "I really appreciate you hanging out, and I really appreciate you keeping an eye on me. I know this place better than you do, I know the houses, hell, and I used to know the people here. I'm going to be fine. I have guns and I know how to use them. It's a five-minute walk up the gravel road. I can't get lost."

"Getting lost isn't what I'm worried about."

"I'm not going to ditch you, Connor. I promised I'd get you back to your brother, didn't I?"

Connor folded his arms across his chest and stared at Aya from the floor. "Forgive me if I don't entirely trust you, given the circumstances."

"Fair point," Aya conceded. "Then how about I leave my bug out bag here as a gesture of good faith? If I don't come back for it by sundown, assume I've been compromised and go on without me."

Connor sighed in defeat. "What are you going to look for?"

"Food, guns, and a car."

"Are you sure you don't want me to come with you?"

"Yeah," Aya said, checking her handgun before choosing a shotgun from the pile of weapons they'd collected. "I need some time to myself. I just need to get my head back in the game. I'll be back in like half an hour, I promise."

Connor sighed again and nodded, there was no use arguing with Aya, she'd made up her mind. Aya flashed him a smile and left the house through the side door. Connor peered around the empty room and then up at the blinking camera. He shook his head and got up to wash the dishes. He promised himself that he'd have a look around the house after, maybe he could find something else useful before Aya got back, and before the 4 hour alarm that was ticking away on his wrist device would finish counting down.

Aya walked slowly. Not because she was worried about startling anything out of hiding, but because she was having a hard time reconciling herself with the fact that she was back in her childhood home. This time, she was fighting for her life, instead of just doing what her parents wanted. It was a kick in the guts that she hadn't been prepared for, and it was taking all of her strength to keep her poker face intact in front of Connor. She didn't want him to know what she was thinking, or that she was really just one bad thought away from breaking down and not getting up. She wasn't even fighting for herself anymore. She was fighting for Connor. He needed her more than she needed him, and she would do everything in her power to make sure that he, at least, got out of the Rapture.

Aya shook her head, forcing herself to clear away her thoughts and keep the tears at bay. Her head was nowhere near the game, it was somewhere off before the zombies had risen, back when she would run through the sprinkler and play with her dog, back when her father was still alive and they'd tend to the huge garden together. Her mind was long gone, back to the fear when they fled the farm because the military was moving in, back to when the dead were coming to life and there was nothing anyone could do once they were bitten.

"Stop dwelling on the past, Aya, it's not going to help you," she chided herself.

The farm she was headed to was just downy he road, it was maybe a five minute walk from the driveway of her family home. She stopped on the edge of the property and stood, staring. She had no fondness for this place, the family who had lived there was not the nicest family. They neglected their animals and were glorified trailer trash. One of the men had been convicted sex criminal, but his family had brought him to live out there not he farm where they had children because it was better for them. Aya's mother had never let her go over unattended, and the only time she and her mother would ever go was to gather eggs from the chickens and ducks that they had domesticated. Mrs. Wu had always complained about the chickens, and would always sneak them extra food because they were too skinny and mean. Aya was always afraid of the chickens, they would all follow her as she helped her mother collect eggs from the tiny coop, ganging up on her and pecking quizzically at her shoelaces. They never attacked her, but they still scared her.

Aya had vague memories of her father going over to help them whenever something broke, and she seemed to recall that something broke every other day. She remembered her father bringing home a half-starved border collie when he'd gone to help one of the men who lived on this farm fix a tractor. They had been keeping the poor dog in with their sheep in an enclosure that wasn't big enough for the animals. The dog was scrawny and his fur was matted. Aya fell in love with him in a heartbeat and she helped nurse the dog back to health. Aya remembered her father giving the other men hell for letting the dog suffer, and that he banned the other men from ever coming back to his farm.

Aya shuddered at the memories of the military moving in when the zombies had risen, destroying the idyllic sanctuary of the farm as they arrived, driving families out as the zombies were rising all around them. She couldn't suppress the sight of rows of dead bodies being carted out of the town, left in the sun, in the ditches. She remembered the military men and women coming down from their northern base to make sure that the outbreak was contained. The screams of the dying and grieving filled her ears as she trudged up the forsaken pathway to the neighbour's farm.

The convicted sex criminal had been the first to turn. He'd been bitten in town at the grocery store when everything was falling apart. Aya had seen him staggering down the road, covered in blood. She was already scared of the man, and her father's shouts echoed in her ears, telling her to get away. She ran back to the house and covered her ears as the gunshots rang out across the yard. She'd never been so scared in her life, as she was when the zombies began to rise.

Aya shuddered and shook her head, clearing away the memories. She had a job to do, and those people were long since gone. The infected criminal had killed his family when he turned, and the military wiped the rest of them out when they got back up. They'd cleaned up the houses, disinfected them all and made them safe again. People had eventually moved back in, but Aya's family never returned to their land. They had no need, or want to. The government bought the land off of them and Aya had never expected to come back.

"Funny how things work out," she muttered.

The chicken coop still stood and Aya smiled sadly to herself. The house she remembered had been a converted trailer with several additions. She remembered that the outside had been a horrible sky blue, but that had since been changed and the house was now a dirty kind of cream colour. The door to the house was wide open and there was some dark stain on the wooden steps and Aya sighed in defeat. There was no way she was going into the house. She moved away from the front door, heading toward the rotting woodsheds that were on the side of the house. The pen where the sheep had once been was still there, too. Nothing had changed, except for the colour of the house. She wondered how much of this had been reconstructed just for this event, and how much of it was original. She noticed a slight charring on the side of the house that spread to the wood of the sheep pen and she felt her stomach lurch. She no longer cared about how much had been left untouched. She just wanted to get what she had come for and get out.

Food was out, but Aya was still holding out hope for ammunition in the shed. She moved her shotgun back over her shoulder, letting the strap settle the weight against her shoulder and back, and instead drew the handgun she wore on her hip. She gripped the splintering handle of the shed and pulled, holding her breath as she did.

The door swung open with a creak, surprisingly light and easy to open despite the age and neglect. Aya breathed a sharp sigh of relief as she discovered two vehicles in the shed.

One was a station wagon, and the other was a truck. Aya checked out the station wagon first. There was nothing inside, and no keys. The door was locked.

"Fuck," she growled, kicking the tire before realizing that the tires on the wagon had been slashed, too. "You sons of bitches," she added in impotent frustration. She turned her attention to the truck. It was a rust bucket that looked like it hadn't run in years. She tried the passenger door. It was open.

"Of course it is," Aya muttered. "This is the one that they want me to take. Bastards." The keys were in the glove compartment.

Aya stood in the garage and peered around. A dented red jerry can caught her eye. She walked over to it and picked it up. It was half full. She nodded to herself and set it in the bed of the truck. There was a large wrench, a pair of shears, another axe and a baseball bat. She took all of the tools and put them in the bed of the truck, too. She couldn't be too prepared. She rummaged through the tool drawers, pocketing some fishing wire, some nails, a hammer, and a pocketknife. She found two flashlights and some batteries, but she didn't bother to test them, she felt that she was running out of time. A quick glance at her wrist showed that the countdown was at just under two hours and she felt her heart skip a beat.

Two hours until the zombies were released, or at least until the sedatives that the Controllers had figured out worked on the zombies wore off. Aya didn't know how they did it, but the Controllers had long ago discovered that the zombies could be put into a stasis state with a certain chemical mixture. It had been theorized that it was just lack of heat that did it, but the Controllers neither confirmed or denied it. Aya's mother had suggested that if it was a chemical compound that did it, then they could use it en masse to sedate hordes for easier disposal, but the suggestion had been smothered by paid opposition to her protests. The Controllers, and Alphonse Ritter, were more powerful than anyone had ever really thought, and weren't above spreading their own propaganda to keep the legitimate protests down and out of the news.

Aya finished her scavenging, disappointed that there was no food, and no reason to go into the house - she didn't dare risk it, her guts were telling her that it would be a mess in there, blood, probably a corpse or two to try an unnerve her and make her break. They had enough food to last them until the game was over, and she could still harvest a bit more from the garden if they were careful to watch for zombies.

Aya climbed into the truck and started the engine. It sputtered and coughed and refused to turn over. Aya let a string of Mandarin curses fly before switching over to English. "Poxy son of a flea ridden whore. Rat bastard, zombie fucking, trailer trash assholes!" She slammed her hands against the steering wheel in rage. She growled under her breath and forced herself to calm down, getting angry wouldn't help her. A cursory glance at the bracelet told her she needed to get her act together if she expected to have everything prepared for the hordes to be released. Since no one was getting any information about where the hordes were coming from, she knew that they'd have to be ready to run at the drop of a hat. Aya took another deep breath and said a short prayer to anyone who was listening, and tried to start the truck again.

The engine whined and protested, but it turned over and started. Aya whispered her thanks and backed the rusty truck out of the shed. She carefully drove the truck down the road, not sure how it would handle if she took a turn too fast, or wound up in the ditch, and parked it back in the driveway of her farmhouse. She'd barely gotten out of the cab before Connor was there, shotgun in hand, ready to defend the house. Aya smiled and waved but her good mood evaporated as she saw the ashen colour of Connor's face.

"What happened?" Aya asked. "Are you hurt?"

Connor shook his head. "There's something you've gotta see, and you're not going to like it."

CHAPTER FOURTEEN

Escape Plan

The ground was damp where she sat but she didn't really care. She'd already stumbled and tripped a couple of times, her jeans were wet, what was a little more wetness added to the mix. She sighed and took off her leather jacket and used it as a seat instead, at least the leather was waterproof and it would keep her from getting too damp to dry off before sundown. She had no idea where she was besides 'halfway up a goddamned hill' but at least she had managed to get away from the man who had been holding her hostage.

She checked the gun she'd stolen from the man in the city. She wasn't familiar with the style, she thought it might be an AK-47, but she had no idea. It had a single magazine in it, and it wasn't completely full. She didn't like her chances if she ran into a horde.

"I like my chances even less if that crazy cracker son of a bitch comes following me," she told herself out loud.

She leaned back and let the sun warm her face as her stomach growled. She placed a hand against her flat belly and sighed. She hadn't eaten since before she'd woken up as a contestant in the Rapture, and the man who had held her hostage made no attempt to be civil. No one got food or water, despite the fact that there was an abundance of cans in the house where they'd all been held. They'd seen it as they were dragged into the cellar. The man in the town hadn't given them a name; he'd given no indication that he was anything but insane. He had ambushed Chloe, and the stories she got from the others were scarily similar. He had broken into houses, armed to the teeth and shouting obscenities as they had woken up from the drugs. Chloe was the only one who had already been awake when he found her, scavenging for food. The others weren't beaten as badly as she had been, but she had been the only one who had really fought back.

The others.

The other players, his hostages.

She shuddered at the thought.

"I couldn't have done anything," she told herself. "Chloe, you know that they'd have done you in. There was no way you'd have been able to save them all. And even if you could have killed that one man, who's to say that the others weren't just as crazy? You know the rules in this game; it's every player for themselves. That man was an executioner and you just escaped Auschwitz."

She shuddered again. Chloe knew that the others she had left were as good as dead, and it was her own fault. She'd been selfish and scared and she'd run. She had a gun, she'd taken their captor's own gun and she could have used it on him, but she didn't. She couldn't kill another person. Zombies were one thing, they were dead. She'd never shot someone before, and she had failed those other people. "All that blood is on your hands now, Chloe."

She could hear her mama chiding her in her southern drawl. How she didn't raise a coward of a daughter. How she ought to be ashamed of herself. Hot tears welled up in her eyes and she let herself cry, salt stinging her dry cheeks as the sun beat down on her. She sobbed until her chest heaved and her lungs hurt. She was exhausted, hungry and thirsty. Her leg throbbed in pain and she was hopeless. She looked at the gun she had stolen and she wondered how bad it would just be to shoot herself and get it over with.

"Would you be proud of me, then, Mama?" she asked rhetorically.

She shook her head and forced herself to stand, even through the pain in her leg. She pulled her jacket back on and zipped it up. It was a little bit of protection against a zombie bite, at least. She held onto the gun, finger well away from the trigger.

"Mama didn't raise no fool about guns," she reminded herself. She checked the metal bracelet on her wrist, hoping that she would have more time than she did. She shook her head, dismayed at the amount of time left. She needed to get well away from there, and at least find shelter before the hordes were released. It hadn't been a particularly good day for Chloe, but she'd be damned if she was going to sit on her ass, feeling sorry for herself.

With dogged determination, she forced herself to continue onward, up the hill out of City Two and the hell away from Agent Seven.

--

"Why the hell is there no food in this damned city?" Topher complained as he and Radek left yet another house. "Not even the grocery store had anything edible left. I swear to God, the Controllers are just pissed off at me and they're doing this out of spite."

"Yeah, that smell has pretty much put me off food for the rest of the week anyway," Radek teased. "Chew some gum. It'll help."

"That's an old wives' tale," Topher complained, as he unwrapped a piece of gum anyway. It was better than nothing, and at least the sugar would keep his spirits up.

Radek sat on the concrete front steps of the house they had just raided and pulled out a map he had pilfered from the gas station they'd torched the day before. It was small, local map but it showed the town they were in, the other town nearby, and listed the amenities of each.

"We haven't checked the drugstore yet," Radek pointed out.

"I'm not really in the mood to risk it," Topher replied with a sigh. "Not after the nastiness we found in the grocery store, and the pizza joint was a bust, too."

"There's a library?" Radek offered. "Get you a book to read tonight?"

"Where's the library?"

"On top of the community centre," Radek replied.

"Ooh, yeah, no," Topher sighed with a shrug. "That's probably where the other zombie horde is."

"How many hordes do they usually have?"

Topher shrugged. "Depends on the size and location of the playing field. Usually there's five or six, but I've seen them use as many as ten smaller hordes."

"You pay a lot of attention to the broadcasts?"

"Uh... Yeah, something like that," Topher said with a curt nod. "It's been going on so long, all the information is online if you look. It's not even like it's particularly hard to find or anything."

Radek gave him a sideways look that said he didn't quite believe him, but he let the subject drop.

"I'm still fucking starving," Topher whined.

Radek laughed. "All right, mister know-it-all. What do you think we ought to do? We don't have very much time left until the horde is released, and if there's still one in this town, we likely won't stand a chance."

Topher made a whining noise in his throat. "I don't know, I'd be just as happy locking myself up in a room on the second floor of a building and waiting for the helicopters to come get us."

"They said they're changing the rules, remember?" Radek pointed out. "We don't know how far that goes."

"They can't leave us if we're still alive and unbitten," Topher argued. "That would be a reason to have the whole damn thing shut down forever and Aya would win her protests."

Radek smirked. "Yeah, that would be good though."

"If Aya won?"

"If her message got through at last."

"How are you so calm and collected?" Topher asked, finally. "I'm starving and half tempted to cook my shoes, or eat my own arm, and you're just sitting here, quiet and calm as ever, it's like you're not even hungry."

"I fast on a regular basis," Radek replied with a shrug. "This is nothing to me."

"You're that kind of religious, huh?" Topher muttered.

"Yes, I'm that kind of religious. I take it you're not?"

Topher shrugged. "Not the fasting kind of religious, no."

Radek laughed. "You see? Your spirits are still up, even if you don't think they are."

"So what's the plan? I'll eat your arm if you're not going to be using it."

"I think we should climb into the truck and start heading out of here. If you think there's another horde, and there's no more weapons or food to be had, then maybe we'll have better luck on the outlying farms that are around here?"

Topher sighed and looked at his bracelet device. "Yeah, I guess that's a better idea than holing up upstairs and hoping for the best."

"There's still eight players around here somewhere," Radek pointed out. "That one guy we saw running, Aya Wu, and God knows who else. Maybe we'll find someone who will be willing to share some food with us, and maybe we'll get out of here with a new friend?"

Topher shook his head and offered his hand to Radek, pulling the other man to his feet. "You're the worst player the Rapture has ever seen. You're too damn calm and collected for this shit."

Radek laughed, clapped Topher on the shoulder and led the way back to their waiting truck.

--

Agent Seven pushed open the door to the community centre on the edge of the town. It was dark inside, and smelled stale. He wept his flashlight across the halls; the green lockers and tarnished coat hooks catching the light and reflecting it back at him. He grunted and picked up the half of the cinder block by the door that the previous occupants had used to hold the door open during business hours in the summer, placing it against the door so he could make a quick escape if needed. He stood very still in the warm air of the building, listening. The sign outside had boasted a gymnasium, meeting spaces and a bowling alley. He was hoping to find a few more edible things to supplement his already impressive stock.

Agent Seven made his way slowly into the building, holding his breath and listening every few steps. He held his gun limply at his side, unafraid, but unwilling to holster it, just in case. He'd come in from the back entrance, away from the main road. On his left, the bowling alley. That was where there'd be anything edible. Even a few cans of soda or a chocolate bar would be good. A treat to keep his spirits up, a luxury item he was unaccustomed to getting on a regular basis.

He stepped lightly, moving quicker to check the bowling alley. The hairs on his arms were standing on end and he felt like he was being watched. The blinking red lights on the cameras above him told him that he was being filmed, but the unease of someone watching wouldn't go away.

Agent Seven swept his flashlight across the darkened bowling alley, the well-polished lanes glimmered as the light hit, but swallowed up the light in other places. Agent Seven stopped a few feet away from the door and looked down.

He'd found a horde of sedated zombies.

Instinctively, he pulled his shirt up over his face. No one knew what kept the zombies sedated, but it was theorized that it was airborne, and could do long-term damage to a living body. Agent Seven wasn't interested in damaging his lungs anymore than he had to, but he realized that the theories about extreme temperatures had just been thrown out the window. He shone his flashlight over the concession. The light caught a few wrappers and Agent Seven weighed his options. One of the zombies on the floor twitched and Agent Seven checked his wrist device. He had time, he decided.

Besides, who in their right mind would say no to a chocolate bar in the middle of the Rapture?

CHAPTER FIFTEEN

Chloe

Her mama didn't raise no fool.

Too bad her mama didn't make it past the apocalypse.

Chloe had seen too much death and destruction in the beginning of the apocalypse. She didn't care for it. She'd lost her taste for survival a long time ago, but luck had always seemed to be on her side and she'd always come out on the better end of things, even when everyone else around her was dying. She wasn't a fighter by any means, she wasn't even sure how to use the gun that her mother had insisted she take from the closet when the dead began to rise, but she did as her mother said because she wasn't foolish enough to think that she would be able to get out of the apocalypse unscathed.

Chloe was a cook. She was the head chef at a five-star catering service. She knew how to filet a fish with her eyes closed but she had no idea how to handle the fact that the dead were coming back to life and eating the living. She could make a pie with a light and flaky crust and the most intricate and beautiful latticework top without breaking a sweat, but the thought of fighting her way out of a horde of the undead made her squirm. She would much rather curl up on the couch with a blanket, a cup of tea, and a book, than go party. She had no idea how to survive without the modern comforts she'd grown so used to. Fighting for her life against zombies, of all things, wasn't exactly how she'd imagined she would end up.

Somehow, Chloe had found herself swept up in a sort of resistance. A group of people who were fighting against the hordes and calling for the government to get off their lazy asses and actually *do something*. She hadn't agreed to help them, but they offered her food and protection in those first days, and considering that between the fact that she had no idea how to survive or shoot a gun, and how broken she was over the horror of watching the fever take her mother, who she'd thought had been so strong and fiery and immortal, Chloe was not cut out for arguing with a mob. It gave her a strange sense of peace to be running with a group, to have someone else to watch her back.

She didn't mind taking the long night watches, and they let her keep her gun, though the group preferred it if she'd stay armed with a melee weapon, and Chloe didn't argue.

She went through hell for six weeks while the world sorted itself out around her, impassive and unable to help fix the mess that humanity had found itself in. She'd become the cook for the group she'd been running with, and it gave her a sense of peace and normalcy in the hectic, dirty first weeks of the apocalypse.

Her group was one of the last to be rounded up, relocated and disbanded. Chloe had never been happier to be taken away by the police and escorted back to her home. Chloe didn't look back as the military police drove her back to her old neighbourhood. She'd never thought she could be so relieved to be returning home, even though she knew exactly what horrors waited for her.

She'd been given her old life back. There wasn't much that had changed. The house had stayed the same. The clean up crews had come through and taken away anything that had been considered a biohazard, and someone had even come in a scrubbed the bloodstains out of walls and carpets. The house smelled like bleach and fresh paint when Chloe returned, but nothing had been damaged and all the canned and dry goods had been left in their respective cupboards. There was even a messily handwritten note detailing everything that had been cleaned and tallied and organized, so that the Resident of this house didn't have to worry about contamination.

Chloe felt nothing after the first wave of relief faded. There was nothing for her to feel. She was empty, and she recognized that it was partly grief and mostly shock. Nothing was the same, she could still see the blood spatter from where she'd been forced to shoot her mother's reanimated corpse, even though they'd cleaned and painted and there was nothing there. She knew it had been there, and she knew what she had done. She couldn't erase that. No amount of bleach could ever scrub that away.

Chloe laughed to herself, her knees giving out as she sank to the floor in the living room. The laughter turned into choked sobs and tears ran down her face as the gravity of the situation began to rear its ugly head and make her question everything about her life. She still had the gun. It was tucked into her purse. She knew that she was a terrible shot, but putting the barrel of a gun in your mouth and pulling the trigger was a sure fire way to end it, wasn't it?

Sobbing, Chloe looked at her handbag over by door. It was so close; all she had to do was cross the living room and grab it. She could put an end to the coldness; to the suffering and to the horror she'd been enduring with one quick decision.

She shook her head.

Her mama didn't raise no fool.

Chloe wiped the tears away from her face and forced herself to get back up. No, things were going okay for her. Her mother had passed the way so many old people do; complications from a violent round of the flu. It was normal for old people to die, she reminded herself. There was nothing she could have done to prevent it. The hospitals would have only prolonged her suffering. It was better; she got to pass relatively peacefully and in her own home.

At least, that was the lie that Chloe would tell herself for the next years following the first outbreak. It was the lie that she forced herself to believe to keep her going. It was the lie that she maintained on a daily basis to keep herself from cracking and breaking down every time she walked back into the door. She forced herself to forget that she had been the one to pull the trigger. She forced herself to forget that the walls and floor had been coated with slick red and black. She forced herself to forget the echoing of the gun that haunted her. She chose to believe that her mother was just old, a victim of the flu that had killed so many people. The zombies were a secondary event that happened to coincide.

It wasn't a perfect lie, but it kept her going long enough to keep from losing her mind.

Chloe was able to return to work two weeks after she returned to her house. The apocalypse didn't destroy everything as badly as Chloe had thought and life returned mostly to normal within two months, at least for her, from the time she was picked up and taken home. She couldn't bear the thought of the people whose lives had become living day to day on the streets with slim pickings for homes, dodging zombies at every turn. Things would normalize for them, too, she told herself. The military would control it, the government would make sure that people were picked up and relocated. They had to.

The lies were all she had, and the lies were what were going to get her through. Chloe stopped watching the news. She cancelled her cable subscription and while she needed to keep her computer and the internet for her business, she never bothered to check anything outside of her emails. The lies she told herself were fragile things, as easily crushed and destroyed as a butterfly in a careless child's hand.

Catering was still a massive business. People were trying to make the best of a horrible situation. Businesses were throwing parties to welcome their surviving staff back to work and wakes and memorial services were being held almost daily it seemed. There was no shortage of high-profile contracts for Chloe to take, and her co-workers didn't question it, either. They kept their heads down and provided the same meals that they had been providing before the dead took over the world.

Chloe noticed the first people dressed in military formalwear at a non-military function three weeks before the scheduled Rapture. She eyed them suspiciously; the military dress wasn't the standard uniforms that she was used to seeing. She'd catered a lot of military mourning receptions over the past few years since the apocalypse. She was pretty sure that she'd seen every type of formal military dress that the city had to offer. International military had been at almost every function; the world was more together in mourning than they ever had been in the past. There was something to be said for tragedy to bring people together.

The unfamiliar military made Chloe uneasy. There was no reason for them to be there, it was a private function and when she asked the guests, no one knew why they were there, or who they were.

Paranoia crept into Chloe's heart, slowly replacing the dead coldness she felt with a sense of dread. She ignored them the first time she saw them, what else could she do? They were there for some reasons she didn't know and it wasn't her place to go and start an incident because she felt like they were there watching her specifically.

Part of her wondered if this was blowback finally catching up to her from the first days in the apocalypse when she'd thrown her hat in with the wrong people. She wondered if she would finally be tried for crimes against the world for the few zombies she'd actually managed to put down.

A sick knot twisted her stomach into a sour, burning knife.

Were they here to put her on trial for killing her mother?

The lies she had been telling herself to keep her mind from breaking suddenly all crumbled away and her chest constricted in fear. She was certain that she was going to throw up and make a mess of the event she was catering.

The second time she saw them, fear took over. She turned the other way and ran as far as could, taking turns and alleys that she normally wouldn't, anything to stay away from the people in the strange military uniforms. She came to rest outside an electronics shop that had big screen televisions blasting the news in the windows. The feed was interrupted by a flashy screen with cut out letters, bright colours and distracting pop music. Chloe couldn't help but be mesmerized. This wasn't news, this was propaganda.

The screen changed to two very young correspondents, dressed like teen pop stars and grinning.

"Welcome to your Rapture!"

Chloe's heart sank as the screen changed to show footage from previous games. Despite not immersing herself in current events, she knew perfectly well what the Rapture was, and the screen flashed several times to show agents dressed exactly like the strange military people she'd seen at her catering event, and then hovering around outside her neighbourhood. They had been following her. She felt somehow relieved at the fact that she wasn't going to be put on trial for crimes committed during the apocalypse, and that she wasn't going to be tried for killing her mother.

The relief was short-lived.

She was so entranced by the flashing imagery on the television screen, so caught up in the strange hype that they had put into promoting the brutal so-called game that was the Rapture, that she didn't notice the agents coming up behind her, pressing their way through the small crowd that had assembled to watch the propaganda.

Chloe didn't notice the fear and silence pass over the group of people as the agents stalked their prey. The Taser hit her just above her waist. She groaned and blacked out, falling back into the arms of the waiting agents. Chloe wasn't even conscious to see her face appear as the lottery winners for the year were being slowly profiled.

CHAPTER SIXTEEN

Goodbye Homestead

"Don't freak out," Connor warned as he led Aya into the house.

"Oh, but when you say that, it makes me want to freak out even more," Aya replied.

"Before I show you what I found, I want to tell you that I've already harvested a bunch more vegetables and stuff from the garden and I've cleaned it all up as best as I could. I even found some old yogurt containers and a couple of mason jars with lids that I washed out, so we could probably store some stuff in them if you want. I was thinking we could put some cooked food in the yogurt containers and use the mason jars to carry water. I just... don't know how much time we're gonna have to prepare anything."

"You're rambling," Aya pointed out.

"I know," Connor replied, making his way around their makeshift beds in the living room. "It's what I do when I'm nervous."

"I make you nervous?"

"I'm more worried about how you're gonna react to this."

Aya eyed Connor as he stopped in front of the root cellar doorway. The root cellar was situated at the end of the hallway, around the corner from the kitchen and right next to the smaller of the main floor bedrooms.

"That's a root cellar," Aya pointed out. "Unless it's been modified, it'll have dirt walls and a rickety-ass wooden staircase. There should be a big kind of box thing dug into the wall, with two sides made up of plywood and some plywood shelves on all the walls and under those rickety-ass stairs. There'll be a single bare bulb, if it's not broken, but that doesn't matter since we haven't got electricity. It's small and uncomfortable down there. Why are you showing me this?"

"I was curious, mostly," Connor replied slowly, pulling a cell phone from his pocket and activating the camera's light to use as a flashlight. He handed the phone to Aya. "I went down there to look, and you have to see what's down there. Please don't freak out."

Aya took the phone and gave Connor a worried look. Connor opened the door and gestured for her to have a look inside the root cellar. Aya stepped forward and the familiar smell of earth and potato rot washed over her. It was colder than she remembered, though, and there was a lingering odour beneath the usual root cellar smell that she couldn't quite place, but that her brain knew wasn't supposed to be there. Slowly, Aya took a step down, then another, and finally a third, stopping halfway down the stairs as the light from Connor's phone illuminated a scene that Aya couldn't have imagined even in her nightmares.

"Oh, God... no."

The root cellar was filled with zombies. They were unconscious and piled up on top of each other like corpses in a mass grave. They would have no problem getting up the stairs, they were piled high enough to simply climb over one another and crawl up the few stairs to get out of the cellar.

A low groaning noise escaped Aya and her hands began to tremble, shaking the phone and making the beam of light waver. Connor was quick, he stepped into the root cellar and managed to wrap his arm around Aya's waist as her knees buckled and she nearly fell down the stairs.

Connor pulled her close, lifting her up just enough to pull her up the stairs. He closed the door with his foot and let Aya go. She leaned against the wall and slowly sank to the floor, shaking.

"I'm sorry," Connor said, kneeling in front of Aya. "I thought it would be best that you know."

Aya leaned forward and drew her legs up to her chest. She rested her head and arms against her knees as her shoulders shook in long silent sobs. Connor moved to sit with her, draping one arm around her shoulders and holding her close until she was able to regain her focus.

"How much of that breakdown of mine got on camera?" Aya asked hoarsely, wiping tears and snot on her sleeve without a thought.

"None, I don't think," Connor replied. "You okay?"

"Not really."

"Of course not, stupid question," Connor sighed. "What do you wanna do about that?"

Aya sniffled and rubbed her eyes. "Fuck, I don't know."

"I have more bad news," Connor added.

"Really?"

"I went to get more wood, thinking that we ought to make sure we have enough supplies, and I checked that barn out there?"

"There's another horde sleeping in there, isn't there?" Aya asked, deadpan.

"Yeah, and we've got about forty-five minutes to decide what we want to do before the timer goes off."

"Fuck."

"Choice is yours, love. This isn't my family home."

Aya ran her hands through her hair, groaning in despair. "I found a truck, some tools, and a bit of gas, although I don't know if it's gonna work in the truck."

"All right, you wanna go down there and smash in zombie heads with a shovel?"

"There's too many of them."

"Well, they're in a basement," Connor pointed out. "I thought that they couldn't do stairs?"

"Yeah, but you saw how many of them are down there. They'll climb over each other and get out."

"Do you wanna barricade the door and hope for the best?"

"Not with a second horde out there in the fucking barn," Aya sighed and shook her head. "No, Connor, I hate to say it, but we're pretty massively fucked right now. We can't stay here."

Connor nodded. "Okay. Shall I start packing things up? Fill the jars with water? At least, if we take the pots and stuff, we can cook over a fire, and a bit of water might come in handy for that, yeah?'

Aya nodded. "Yeah, let's pack up."

"Then what?" Connor asked.

Aya gave Connor a look, a mad gleam in her eyes. Connor didn't ask where she was going when she got up, he just hurried and packed up as much extra food as he could manage and started hauling supplies out to the truck.

Aya returned with the dented red jerry can and a box of matches.

"We've got about twenty minutes," Connor announced.

Aya nodded. "Can you haul the twin mattress into the bed of the truck? At least we can give ourselves something comfortable to sleep on if we have to camp out, and we'll be off the ground."

"Yeah, no problem," Connor replied, eyeing Aya nervously. She was speaking in a quiet monotone and it was worrying him. "Anything else you think we need?"

Aya shook her head. "No, I don't think there's much else we need. You've got the food and the cookware?"

"And the mason jars filled with water, yeah. Our bug-out bags are already in the truck, and I grabbed the last cans of food that we were gonna leave out of the bags and tossed them in the truck, too."

"Good."

"What are you going to do?"

"I'm going to have a bonfire."

Connor cringed. "Okay, wait for me before you light this place up," he said. "And give me the matches. There's a perfectly good fire in the stove."

Aya handed Connor the matches and he pocketed them before lifting the mattress. He maneuvered himself out the small side door and Aya could hear him cursing as he stumbled over the dip in the grass he'd forgotten about.

Aya turned to look at the cameras. "Nice try, you son of a bitch," she drawled. "I ain't broken yet."

Connor returned and opened the stove. "Okay, go dump some gasoline down on those poor rotting bastards in the cellar. Try not to spill any on the stairs. We'll dump some on the couches when we grab up the pillows and blankets on our way out, and toss a scoop of embers on them, okay?"

Aya nodded and gathered up the pillows they'd slept on the night before into a pile in the middle of the blankets they'd used. "Easier to grab," she offered with a shrug. Connor smiled and nodded his approval.

Aya made her way back to the root cellar and dumped half of the gasoline on the slumbering zombies, following Connor's instructions and being careful not to spill. She walked back into the living room and grabbed up the bundle of pillows and blankets by gathering up the corners. She made a point to flip the camera the bird one more time.

"Burn it down," she commanded.

Connor nodded and pulled a burning log out of the fire. He walked quickly to the root cellar as Aya carried the blankets out to the waiting truck.

Connor followed shortly and Aya sat in the idling truck, jaw set as tears welled up in her eyes but she refused to let them fall. Connor opened the passenger door and set the jerry can down in the back seat before climbing in.

"The barn next."

Connor nodded and shut the door. He was worried about Aya, her voice was cold and flat, and her eyes were lifeless. She'd gone cold, something Connor had seen far too many times in his past work. The last time he'd seen his brother get cold like that, it didn't end well, and Connor wasn't sure that Aya would be able to get over the shock. Aya drove across the front yard, ignoring the orange flames that licked the plywood boarding up the windows of her childhood home. She drove the truck carefully and parked it near the barn.

"Do you wanna do the honours?" Connor asked.

Aya shook her head. Connor grunted and got out of the truck, taking the jerry can with him. He didn't mind doing the dirty work. He was impressed that Aya had been able to burn the house down in the first place, and was even more impressed with the fact that she'd been able to drive across the lawn. He hurried himself, trying not to take too much time. Aya was on the very edge of going into shock and he didn't want to leave her side for too long if he could help it. She didn't really have any other outlet for her frustration and shock would mean that she wasn't going to be paying as much attention to their surroundings. They were in it together now for real.

Aya watched as Connor went in the side door and disappeared. She chewed on her thumbnail as she waited, wishing that the radio would work, or that there was a tape in the old truck's tape deck, anything to get her mind off the job that Connor was doing. She got out of the car as Connor came running out of the barn like a bat out of hell. Whatever else had been in the barn aside from the zombies had caught on fire really fast, and hot orange flames crawled over the dry wood of the barn's exterior. The wails of burning zombies filled the air, a symphony of groans and tortured screaming. Aya stumbled backward before turning around and throwing up. She managed to keep her balance as she retched, emptying her stomach onto the dry ground. Connor retrieved a Mason jar of water for her as he approached and she waved it away, coughing and spitting.

"Can you drive?" Aya asked, her voice hoarse.

"Yeah."

Aya spit on the ground once more and reached for the water Connor was still holding. She gargled, rinsed her mouth and spit it all back out onto the dirt, trying to ignore the sounds of zombies burning to death in her family barn. Connor helped her up into the truck before climbing into the driver's seat and starting the engine.

"Where do you want to go?"

"Down the highway," Aya said. "Away from here and away from where we heard the explosions."

"Okay. Are you okay?"

"Sure."

Connor nodded and didn't say anything else as he gently pulled the truck away from the fires and drove out into the field where there was a dirt mound passing over the ditch usually used for large farm equipment and trucks used for herding cattle to pull off the highway and into the field.

Aya stared forlornly out the window as Connor drove them away from the burning farm. They sat in silence and Aya rested her head against the cold glass of the window, trying not to be too broken-hearted over the loss of the home that hadn't been hers in a long time.

A bang broke Aya's distraught reverie and Connor let fly a string of curses as he forced the truck to pull over on the wrong side of the road.

"Oh what the hell?" Aya muttered.

Connor's face was pale and he got out of the truck, still swearing.

"What?" Aya asked, following Connor out of the cab of the truck.

Connor popped the hood and was greeted with a face full of hot white steam.

"That's not good, is it?" Aya asked.

"Fucking radiator," Connor swore. "I think? Could be a bunch of stuff, but that steam? Likely the rad."

Aya groaned and felt her stomach heave again. She leaned against the side of the truck and closed her eyes, praying that she wasn't about to throw up. Again.

"I can try to put some water in the radiator, and hope that it'll work long enough to get us to that other town you were talking about?" Connor suggested. "But I can't promise that this rust bucket is gonna start again or run for more than a few more kilometres."

"Fuck," Aya groaned. "There's nowhere else to go. I don't know any of the other houses, unless we head back toward the farm. I mean... there are a couple houses there but we did just start a damned wildfire and we can't know how many zombies are escaping that. I dunno what to do. You got any ideas?"

"How far to the other town?"

Aya shrugged and shook her head. "I dunno. Ten kilometers maybe? But it's down a big hill, trees on either side and nowhere easy to hide if things get worse."

"We could just camp out here, sleep in the truck and pray for the best? You sleep now, I'll watch, we switch in a couple hours when I can't keep my eyes open?"

Their discussion was interrupted by the sound of a honking horn. Aya and Connor exchanged looks and turned to face the direction they'd just come from. Another truck, taller and in better shape than the one they'd stolen was speeding toward them down the highway. Aya's gun was in her hand before she realized it and she took careful aim at the truck, just in case. Connor eyed her carefully, but didn't say anything. She wasn't trigger happy, just cautious and he couldn't fault her for that. Her finger wasn't on the trigger and Connor silently applauded her gun safety. The truck rolled to a gentle stop and the window unrolled.

"Hey, don't shoot! You guys need a hand?" the driver asked.

The passenger leaned over the driver and flashed Aya a smile. "Yeah, we can help you, no problem. Happy to, but also, do you guys have any food? We're starving."

CHAPTER SEVENTEEN

Dynamic Duos

"What do you think?" Connor asked quietly, leaning over to whisper in Aya's ear.

"I don't trust anyone," Aya replied.

"Not even me?"

"Special circumstances."

"So these guys?"

Aya gave a one-shouldered shrug.

"Look," the darker of the two men said. "I know you don't have any reason to trust us, we're contestants in this shitshow, just like you, and we've been known to blow things up when we're frustrated."

"And we've been frustrated for a couple hours now."

Connor chuckled mirthlessly and nodded his agreement. "It's been a frustrating day, that's for sure. You guys got names or what?"

They two men introduced themselves as Radek and Topher.

"You're the guys who blew up the other city?" Connor asked.

"Yeah," the darker coloured Radek replied with a sheepish grin. "You the guy we saw running like hell when we all woke up?"

Connor nodded.

"So who are you?" Radek asked.

"I'm Aya Wu, this is Connor," Aya replied.

"Wow, Aya, it's an honour to meet you," Radek said.

Aya nodded, speechless. She didn't know what to do when people treated her like a celebrity. "Thanks for offering your help."

"Hey, no problem," Topher said with another smile. "We're not in this to kill the competition."

Aya nodded again.

"Did you two set that fuckin' fire back there?" Topher continued. "There was like a house and a barn and everything was starting to spread. Looked like a horde was there?"

"Yeah," Connor interrupted quickly. "We set it, there were two hordes. Then the truck broke down and here we are."

Radek nudged Topher with his elbow. It was their sign to shut up.

"Sorry we're so blunt," Radek said, changing the subject. "We had no food. We got some water, and some Gatorade and a chocolate bar. There was nothing to eat in that whole damned town."

"Well," Topher interrupted, "we ate the beef jerky."

"You ate the beef jerky," Radek corrected.

Aya chuckled. "We've got food."

"You wanna share?" Topher asked. "Maybe curl up next to a bonfire and share some body heat?"

Aya shrugged again, scowling at the blatant come on, but lowered her gun. "Let me talk it over with my partner, you mind?"

"By all means," Radek agreed. "Thanks for not shooting us on sight."

Aya smiled coldly. "It's a small mercy I guess. You're welcome."

Connor followed as Aya walked away from the two strange men in the truck. Neither looked back as they wandered just out of earshot.

"At least they didn't shoot us in the back," Connor muttered.

"Honestly, Connor? There was a part of me that was hoping they'd just make this a mercy killing and let us out of the fucking game."

Connor looked Aya over, his lips pressed into a thin line of worry and dismay. "Really?"

"I'm tired and I don't have it in me to keep going."

"Since when?"

"Since we burned down my house."

"That wasn't your house anymore," Connor pointed out. "You know that. You know that the Controllers are just doing this all to fuck with you, why are you letting it get to you now?"

"I'm not as strong as you think I am."

"Yes you are."

Aya looked up at Connor and forced a weak smile. "You're way too good to be here."

"What about those guys?" Connor asked, ignoring the blatant compliment. "What do you want to do about them?"

"Kill them in their sleep?"

"Really?"

Aya snorted a bitter laugh and shook her head. "I don't know, Connor. What do you want to do about them?"

"Let's weigh our options," Connor suggested. "We can kill them and take their truck, but we dunno where they came from, and if we're gonna believe them, then there's no supplies back where they came from. Plus they set off a bunch of explosions and at least one of them had to have been a gas station."

"Okay, I don't really want to kill anyone," Aya mumbled.

"So then that's not an option," Connor agreed. "And they don't seem like they want to kill us, either, so we can either team up with them, or we can tell them to fuck off."

"Do you think we have enough supplies to share?"

"If we're careful, I don't see why we can't make them last. And it's not like we have much more than maybe thirty-six hours until rescue, right?" Connor reminded. "We can skip high tea if it means stretching our rations a bit farther."

Aya smiled, a genuinely amused smile, and Connor felt relief spread through him like warm cider on a cold day. If she was smiling, she was relaxing. The crisis was passing.

"Okay," she agreed reluctantly. "If you think that they're okay for us to trust, then I will follow your lead on this one."

"Extra eyes, extra hands to hold all those extra guns we have."

Aya nodded. "Okay. I'm in."

Connor placed a kiss on the top of Aya's forehead. "It's gonna be okay."

They smiled as they walked back to the truck where Topher and Radek were waiting. Aya stretched out her hands in a welcoming gesture, as though she was going to give everyone a hug. "Good news," she announced. "We've decided that we should totally team up with you guys because we could use the help."

"Awesome," Topher said, breathing an audible and visible sigh of relief. "Thanks for letting us join you."

"Thanks for not shooting us in the back when we walked away," Aya replied. "That was the first test."

"Really?" Radek asked. "Is there a second test?"

"Yeah," Connor piped in with a smirk. "It's unloading the contents of our truck into yours without breaking anything or getting weird."

Topher laughed and clapped Radek's shoulder. "Come on, Radek, let's earn our dinner."

Aya and Connor had to admit that they were glad they decided that they could use the help. They let the other contestants unload their supplies from the broken down truck and Aya directed them to a flat, treeless spot to pull over and set up a makeshift camp. They drove in silence except for Aya giving her directions in an exhausted monotone. The place Aya picked to camp was a small clearing, in a field left to go fallow. There were trees lining the corner of the lot, thin things planted in dense rows that had been planted by the farmers ages ago in order to act as a windbreak. More copses dotted the field further in, but Aya wanted to camp at the edge of the lot, by the rows where they'd be at least partially hidden from any other passing vehicles, and where they could easily collect firewood. No one argued with her logic and Radek pulled the truck carefully across the path meant for large equipment that bridged the ditch leading to the field. It didn't take long for them to pick a spot to Aya's liking and the four of them climbed out of the truck to take better stock of their surroundings. Topher immediately began pulling bags back out of the bed of the truck and rummaging through them, eager to find something to eat.

"Where the hell did you get fruit and shit?" Topher asked, producing a jar filed with Saskatoon berries and a handful of potatoes.

"We were on that farm you guys said you saw burning," Aya explained with a nonchalant shrug. "There was stuff growing. Don't you know how to forage?" She huffed a sigh and changed the subject. "You got any camping gear?"

Radek shook his head. "All we have is what you see."

"No weapons?" Connor asked.

"I have a crossbow and Radek here has the shittiest rifle I've ever seen."

"What the hell?" Connor asked. "They expect you to fight with your bare hands?"

"They probably expected us to die," Topher replied with a shrug.

"It's a good thing that Topher knows how these Controller guys think. Without the bombs we set off, we'd have been as good as zombie chow," Radek said. "There was nothing to scavenge in that whole city. Everything was looted or rotted."

"And I'm not really one for the outdoorsy type of lifestyle," Topher added.

"Hey, guys?" Aya interrupted. "As much as I would love to sit here all day and get to know you, we need to get some firewood, and get things better organized so that when the sun goes down, we can work out shifts and not get caught by a zombie horde."

Connor saluted casually with two fingers and grinned at the new members of the team. "I'll take Topher, we'll go get firewood, okay?"

Aya nodded and Connor nudged Topher, leading him away from the group.

Radek watched the others go and noticed Aya's immediate reaction. "You're relaxed now, he's been bugging you this whole time. Do you know Topher?"

Aya shook her head. "You're very perceptive. How'd you know he was making me uncomfortable?"

"You haven't been at ease since we picked you up and Topher asked for food."

Aya smiled. "Sorry. He's really familiar and I can't place him. It's bugging me. And the fact that he's been constantly flirting with me? A little annoying."

"I will ask him to stop."

"You don't have to, but I appreciate the sentiment."

Radek smiled. "Suit yourself. What can I do to help you set up a camp?"

Aya kicked the ground, lowering her eyes in tired embarrassment. "Am I really that much of a leader to everyone?"

"Well, you're an honest hero of mine and I strive to be as outspoken as you one day."

Aya took Radek's hand in hers and patted the back of it. "Well then, I'll do everything in my power to get you out of here, too."

Radek nodded and took his hand back. "Do you plan to sleep in the bed of the truck?"

"That's what the mattress is for," Aya agreed. "As long as it doesn't start raining."

"We have a couple tarps in the back of our truck. We could make a couple makeshift lean-tos?"

Aya's face lit up in delight. "Brilliant! I have fishing wire in my bag we can use to string them up. Maybe get a couple of big sticks from the trees around here?"

"Sounds like a plan, then," Radek agreed, moving to pull the tarps out of where they'd stored them inside the truck as Aya headed to the trees near the road to look for long branches or broken trees that they could use as tent poles.

--

Connor and Topher worked in silence, gathering as much deadfall as they could carry, while keeping a close eye out for any hordes of the undead that might be shambling across the fields. Not being given any more announcements made life harder and it was well beyond the allotted four hour reprieve from zombies.

Topher decided to break the silence first. "How do you know Aya?"

Connor eyed the other man. "I didn't until I ran into her on day one. I mean, I knew who she was from the news and stuff, but I'd never met her 'til now."

Topher nodded. "Yeah, me neither. Is she as uh, shall we say, feisty as she is on television?"

Connor shrugged and picked up a long piece of wood, he nonchalantly weighed it in his hand, vaguely wondering if it was too dry and rotten to use as a bludgeoning tool. It was lighter than he'd anticipated, despite being about the length of a baseball bat. "Suppose so? She's kept a pretty level head this whole time. Hasn't done anything that I'd call reckless, despite the fact that the Controllers are doing everything in their power to fuck with her."

"Sounds like the Controllers all right," Topher agreed, though there was a note of discomfort in his voice.

"You shouldn't be hitting on her like that," Connor added, eyeing Topher as he picked up another stick. It wasn't as long as the previous one he'd picked up and he tucked it into his armful with a sigh. "She doesn't need you complicating things. You're lucky she didn't shoot you already."

"Why's that?" Topher asked.

"She hasn't shot anything yet," Connor replied. "She's on edge and needs a way to take out some of this frustration. She just burned down her family home, she's looking for a fight. Don't be a target."

"Oh yeah?" Topher asked, dropping his armful of deadfall. "What's it matter to you if I flirt with her?"

"Fuck off," Connor snapped, ignoring Topher's menacing stance and ready to fight attitude. "We've got things that need to be done and dusted before we can even think about eating or getting any rest and you wanna start a fight? This isn't the time for this macho bravado bullshit."

"Oh, so you like her."

"You really think this is about whether or not I like someone who is probably gonna forget about me as soon as this is all over - and that's even being generous because in all likelihood, we're all as good as dead already no matter what the outcome of this little fucking game is."

"You tellin' me that your whole 'don't flirt with the only woman in the game' attitude isn't macho bravado bullshit? You marking your territory?"

"Marking my territory?" Connor echoed. He snorted derisively. "Sure. I'm marking my territory, but not like that. She's my partner, promised not to shoot me if I helped her. I've helped her so far and I'd like to see this Rapture to the end, and if she's my ticket out, then yeah, I'm gonna do everything in my power to protect me so-called territory."

"Please, as if that's all she is to you now. You've been making eyes at her every time she looks away. I saw that forehead kiss you gave her when you decided whether or not we could join you. As if that's not some sort of twisted affection. You guys sleep together back on the farm? Get a little one-night stand stress relief in before the cameras started rolling? Or are you twisted enough that you didn't even care if the cameras were on?"

"Don't push me," Connor warned. "You don't know what I was before this happened."

"You're one of them Irishmen from Nottingham North, right?" Topher asked.

Connor's face went blank and the colour drained from his already pale skin.

"Yeah, I know who you are, Connor," Topher drawled. "I know who every single person in this game is. I know you've got a brother, and that he's probably calling in all sorts of favours right now. Radek is a peaceful protestor, never done anything particularly violent, but likes to start riots and encourages people to do other things, a little violent if necessary, but never on the front lines himself. He's a slave to Aya's teachings. He wouldn't hurt a fly. Don't think he's ever done anything particularly violent, despite having a military background. Hell, I don't think he'd know how to kill a zombie if it was right in his face. You wanna know who's left in City Two?"

Connor was stunned. "Who the fuck are you?"

Topher grinned, and it wasn't quite a sane look. "I used to be a Controller. This game? This year in particular? This was set up three years ago. You were watched, you were played. You've been picked specifically for this. You just weren't supposed to make it this far."

Connor gripped his armful of wood. "Issat right? Then what did you do to end up here?"

Topher's grin slid from his face and a hunted look that was even less sane replaced it. "I protested this selection."

"Why?"

Topher shrugged. "It was a stupid move. I fought the law, and I paid the price. Spent a year in prison under the watchful eye of the Grand Controller. I was left for dead here. No one would care if I died. Why do you think there were no weapons and no food left in City One? I wasn't supposed to make it this far, but I knew where the hordes were. Managed to destroy two of 'em. Convinced Radek that I could help him get outta this alive if he'd team up with me. I know that there are supplies in City Two, if we can make it. You guys weren't a part of my plan. I'm here to take down the game, in my own way. I'm here to get the fuck out and spit in Alphonse Ritter's god damned face and sell my story to the right people. The Game won't last another five years once I tell the world what the Controllers do behind the scenes. If I gotta flirt with Aya Wu to do it, so be it, and I ain't gonna let you stand in my way."

"You son of a bitch," Connor snarled, dropping the wood he'd collected. He lunged at Topher, grabbing the other man by the front of the shirt.

Topher raised his knee as Connor grabbed him, kneeing the Irishman in the gut. Connor huffed a heavy exhalation of breath, but Topher wasn't strong enough to do much damage to someone who kept himself in as good physical shape as Connor did. Connor swung a punch, catching Topher in the ribcage. Topher grunted and grabbed at Connor, forcing them both to the ground. They landed hard, Connor groaned as Topher landed on top. Topher crowed in triumph as he swung overhand punches down on Connor's head and torso. Connor managed to get his arms up to protect his face from the strikes Topher was aiming at him. Toper was about to throw another punch when a rustling sound stopped the fight. Neither man moved, and silence descended for a long moment.

Another rustle and the sound of something being dragged broke the spell of rapt fear that had taken hold of them.

"Fuck," Topher hissed, scrambling to get up.

Connor grabbed Topher's ankle and dragged him back to the ground as he got up instead. He drew the handgun on his waist and aimed it at Topher. "Stay down, motherfucker."

Topher nodded.

"I'm not gonna kill you," Connor promised. "Stay down and stay quiet. If that's zombies, I'll protect you, as long as you're done being an asshole."

Topher nodded again and crossed his heart.

"I'm holding you to that."

Topher breathed a sigh of relief as Connor stalked off, slowly, moving toward the sound they'd heard. Topher rolled over, ready to get up and run if he needed. Connor moved like a cat stalking his prey, he was in his element, gun held level before him, stalking, silent, unnerved.

"Don't shoot!"

"Fuck," Connor hissed as the woman stood slowly from her hiding spot.

"Please, don't shoot," she repeated. "Here," she tossed her weapon at Connor's feet. "I need help."

Connor holstered his gun. "You hurt?"

"Yeah. But... Uh... Not bit."

"Come on then."

The woman took a hesitant step forward and collapsed. Connor swore under his breath and picked up her gun first, then her.

"Thank you," she muttered as Connor hoisted her bridal style.

"Topher, get up," Connor sneered, aiming a kick at the prone man. "You fucking scaredy cat. What were you gonna do? Run and let me get eaten? Nice. Pick up the wood and let's get back."

Topher nodded and did as he was told, eyeing Connor as he carried the new woman back to camp. Topher, carrying the wood they'd gathered, followed wordlessly. Neither particularly happy about finding yet another survivor. Another person, injured no less, was just going to complicate things even further and they both knew it. They both knew that Aya wouldn't turn her away, and that she wouldn't advocate shooting her, but the unspoken fear of what another person meant to the already strained group dynamic weighed heavily on them both.

CHAPTER EIGHTEEN

Topher

To be perfectly honest, he wasn't even sure how me had managed to get put on the set-up team in the first place. If he was going to be honest with himself, he wasn't even sure how he'd ended up working for The Rapture, either. He wasn't exactly fond of the system. He wasn't a protestor though, either. He was mostly indifferent to it, but it had been paying the bills for years. He was just mostly confused about how he'd managed to get promoted as fast and as far as he had. He wasn't exactly the greatest of workers. He wasn't particularly skilled at anything that would have explained the promotion, either, but here he was.

"Here" was in the field for the third time since he had applied to work in data entry for the Rapture. He didn't exactly know what data entry was supposed to be, but he was good enough that they'd pulled him out and put him in analytics, and then into bookkeeping (which, he found out quickly was making bets on behalf of the Rapture and playing the odds like a bookie) and finally into field work.

Topher was quiet and kept mostly to himself. He didn't necessarily make a lot of friends within the behind the scenes of The Rapture, but he had never really considered that he'd made himself enemies. He had played the statistics game for years and had made the Rapture a lot of money from their bets. He had learned how to rig the game in their favour and ever since he'd moved into fieldwork, the ratings had spiked, thanks to his clever traps and keen eye for potential drama-starters.

It had been Topher's idea to remove most of the food and survival equipment from City One in the upcoming Rapture. He'd never imagined that he'd find himself in the city in a year.

"What do you think you're doing?"

Topher stopped in his tracks, nearly dropping the box of canned goods and electronics that he had carefully packed. He was heading away from the rest of the group, wandering aimlessly to the edge of the town. There was a house he'd been carefully monitoring, filling with supplies and things that would make winning the Rapture a breeze. He had made a safe house in every city he'd visited, and so far, none of the players in any of the Raptures he'd worked on had ever found his windfall. Usually, the players would camp in the middle of the cities, or they'd all go insane and start killing one another. Either way, Topher's safe houses were left alone and he'd never been caught.

Until now.

"I'm taking some canned goods to a couple of the houses on the edge of the city," Topher replied. "Just a couple tins of beans and junk." He shrugged and shifted the weight of the box, hoping that the other field agent wouldn't ask to help. "You know, give the players a bit of hope that maybe they'll find something good."

The other field agent grunted. Topher knew the other man's name was Jake, and that he wasn't the most imaginative of people. He was a drone, assigned to make sure there were cameras placed in prime locations to capture every desperate moment. Jake knew his way around electricity and circuits, and that was about it. He did his job and didn't question morals. According to his personnel file, Jake had been a member of the Program Team since the second year.

Topher thought that he would make an interesting addition to the Rapture one year. Jake was the boring kind of drone who kept the same routine every day and loathed change. He was quiet and didn't socialize. Topher wondered how much pressure it would take for Jake to crack and lose his cool.

Topher would have put a good wager on Jake taking first blood in The Rapture. Jake was anti-social and paranoid enough that one wrong word could send him over the edge. Adding zombies and forced survival into the mix would be just the right level of stress and motivation to get the quieter man to snap.

Topher stood for a long moment, waiting to see if Jake was going to continue talking. When he didn't, Topher grunted to himself and continued on his way. It was the fifth load of food and electronics that he'd taken into the small house on the corner. Jake was the first person to actually stop and ask what he was doing. Topher's guts rolled. Jake might have been unimaginative, but he was also the kind of person who would definitely narc on someone if he thought it would serve him well.

He moved faster, just to avoid Jake looking back at him and changing his mind about how curious he actually was.

The house was quaint, with two steps leading up to the front door. Nothing good enough to stop zombies, but it was better than nothing. Topher wasn't impressed with the huge picture window on the front of the house, but he supposed he couldn't be too picky. After all, it wasn't like he was going to be holing up in the place. It was on the very edge of the town, there was a small drop across the street that ended in a shallow creek. It was away from the main stretches and Jake hadn't installed any cameras on the road leading to the house yet. There weren't any lampposts so Topher assumed that it would be a dead zone anyway. He grinned to himself as he entered the house again. He'd already set up the signal jammers he needed to create a dead zone within the house. Anything that the Rapture Team put inside would not work, and no one would be able to figure out why. He ran upstairs and into the bedroom where he'd been hiding his electrical gear. He placed a satellite phone in the closet and went back downstairs to finish stocking the pantries.

When he was finished, he was satisfied that anyone lucky or clever enough to find his safe house would be able to survive the entire game without ever having to really lift a finger. He'd even stashed a metal ladder that he'd found in the house's backyard shed upstairs. There was rooftop access from the attic, too. The house was perfect in every way, except for the picture window. Topher hated it, thought it was a liability and considered changing the safe house location, but also knew that he really didn't have the time. It would have to do.

When they were finished the backbreaking task of rigging the areas for the upcoming Rapture, they were all loaded back into the vans and debriefed. There was still a year before the game would take place, but things were meant to be prepared well before then. They wouldn't have time to adjust things once the game was scheduled to begin. People needed to be relocated, the playing field was quarantined, and highway traffic would need to be diverted. It was a huge undertaking, to use a previously inhabited place as a Rapture locale, but it would always be worth it in the end. Rural events always had higher ratings than abandoned city events.

Topher looked over his file folder as the vans rumbled on back to the home base. There would be a lot of testing and adjustments made over the next year as players were monitored and rounded up and zombie hordes were brought in from all over. The military presence was quadrupled to ensure that no one got into the game zone. It would be a gruelling year.

Flipping through the paper file, Topher stopped as he looked at the already-chosen contestants files. One name in particular stood out and struck him as something wrong. He said nothing until they were back in their base.

"Excuse me, Mr. Ritter?"

Alphonse Ritter scared Topher. It wasn't the scars, or the height, or the fact that he looked like he would have no problem snapping someone's neck that did it. There was something else about him that just made Topher's blood run cold, and he couldn't place exactly what it was.

"Ah, Topher. It's good to see you. I was worried that you weren't going to come back from this excursion."

Topher forced a smile. "No? Why is that?"

"You always have had a love of rural living, haven't you?"

"I like to be alone," Topher agreed slowly. "And some of the scenery out here is absolutely stunning, but I don't think it's remote enough for me."

Alphonse laughed and Topher felt his guts squirm again. "What can I do for you today?"

"Well..." Topher began slowly; suddenly very aware that what he was asking was highly controversial in and of itself. "It's just that I was looking over the contestants we've got lined up already for next year."

"Ah, excellent," Alphonse replied. "You've always been very good at reading people. What do you think of this year's mix?"

Topher hesitated. "I'm not sure that Aya Wu is such a good idea..."

--

They took him out of his bunker in the middle of the night. There was nothing to stop them and no one heard the commotion. Even if Topher had screamed when they dragged him out of his assigned sleeping quarters, no one would help him. He didn't give anyone the satisfaction of screaming when they threw him in the dark cell. He didn't give anyone the satisfaction of begging until he felt his ribs break under the boots of his captors. He barely made any sound at all as they told him he'd be locked up for a good long while as the Rapture preparations went on without him. He didn't give anyone the satisfaction of making any noise as they made threats on his life. He knew what he had done, but he didn't think the response would have been so extreme. He'd made the mistake of questioning Alphonse Ritter and he was about to pay the price.

He wasn't sure how long he'd been alone in the dark. The ache in his bones and the fact that his clothes didn't fit as well as they'd used to suggested months. He wasn't tortured exactly, but it was solitary confinement with very little human contact. He wasn't even sure that he could talk anymore.

The door opened and light spilled into the room. Topher squinted and rolled over from where he'd been sleeping. Standing in the light was a familiar body that made Topher's blood run cold. It was Alphonse Ritter himself.

"Hello, Topher," Alphonse crooned. "I have a proposition for you."

CHAPTER NINETEEN

(Un)Welcome Guests

By the time Topher and Connor returned, Aya and Radek had set up a tarp lean-to, tied one tarp over the bed of the truck where Aya's mattress was, and had started a fire. They were preparing food when the boys returned.

"I brought a stray," Connor announced.

Aya gave Connor a weary thumbs up but said nothing.

"I brought more firewood, but it looks like it's almost redundant since you two are a lot more efficient than we were."

"There's something to be said about having people who know how to follow instructions without question," Aya said. "People who take the initiative to grab things that might be helpful. We set up the damn tents in less than ten minutes. Seemed logical to try and have a fire started before you guys got back considering we were closer."

"Sorry we took so long," Connor replied.

"I can see why it took you so long," Aya said, eyeing the newcomer and giving Connor a questioning look.

Connor didn't say anything and surreptitiously shook his head as he passed, a silent promise to explain things when they got a chance to talk in private. Aya bit her lower lip but didn't say anything. She wasn't happy about having another mouth to feed and another person that she wasn't sure she could trust. As anticipated, however, Aya wasn't about to turn the newcomer away. It was obvious that she was either injured or too weak to fight since Connor had carried her back to the camp, and Aya's conscience wouldn't let her turn someone asking for help away. She knew they'd have enough supplies, but now there were three reasons to sleep with one eye open and Aya wasn't sure that she could handle the emotional and mental stress of it. Even with Connor on her side.

"Dinner will be ready in a few minutes," Radek announced as Connor set the woman down on the ground near the fire. "It's nothing fancy, but at least it's warm."

"Anything is better than nothing at this point," the new woman replied. "I haven't eaten since I arrived here, and I thank you sincerely for your hospitality."

"No problem," Connor replied with a shrug. He offered a wan smile, his exhaustion finally starting to show. He shot a cold glare at Topher as he passed, and went to sit quietly with Aya, stretching out his long legs with a groan under his breath as he let the warmth of the fire work its way into his tired body.

"My name is Chloe, thank you for taking me in."

"I'm Radek, that's Aya," Radek replied. "You've met Connor and Topher."

"Her leg is messed up," Connor said slowly, "but she's not bit."

"I was attacked by a crazy man," Chloe said simply. "He took hostages. I think he might have killed them? I don't know. There were at least three others. Maybe five of us all together? I didn't count them. I woke up after being drugged and dragged to this godforsaken place with a gun in my face." She shuddered. "The man is crazy, I tell you. I tried to fight him off the first time and he hobbled me. He forced us into a basement of a house somewhere. There were canned goods all stacked up, but none of them were the kind you could open without a can opener. It was like a taunt. Like he was telling us to look at all the food he had, but that we weren't getting any of it."

"Where was this?" Topher asked, worriedly.

"In the little town down the hill that way," Chloe replied, pointing vaguely in the direction she'd come from. "We were kept in the basement while the drugs worked out of our systems. Then he dragged us all out into the streets, one by one." She crossed herself and shook her head. "God help me, he build some kind of traps all over. I don't know, I was scared and I was positive that I was going to die there, at his hand."

"Shit," Radek breathed.

Chloe nodded. "I'm no hero. God help me, I ran. I saved my own skin like a coward. I left those poor people to die..."

"You did what you had to do," Connor reassured her. "No one can hold that against you."

"Do you even know how to shoot?" Radek asked.

"Not really," Chloe admitted. "I... I've used a gun before, sure. We all did what we had to do when the Rising happened, right?"

"We did," Radek agreed.

Chloe laughed, a bitter and mirthless sound in the slowly darkening twilight. "I'm a shit shot though."

That comment lightened the mood and a smattering of laughter rippled through the rest of the group. The tension eased enough and even Connor was able to breathe a sigh of relief.

"Welcome to the group," Aya replied. "We'll help you as much as we can."

"Don't be too offended if we don't offer you a gun back," Connor teased.

Chloe laughed and shook her head. "I won't be, I wouldn't want me using a gun around a group either."

"Well, we'll do what we can to keep you safe," Aya promised. "And we might give you a smaller gun, just in case."

"I appreciate it, really," Chloe replied. "If you like, I'll cook the morning meal. It's kind of what I used to do."

"Sorry I wasn't able to make these beans and canned spaghetti more fancy," Radek joked as he gave the pots a final stir.

"Thank God there's only a day left," Topher added. "I dunno if I can ever look at a tin of beans the same way again."

"You were practically begging for beans like an hour ago," Aya pointed out. "But I'm mostly happy to know there's only a day left because surviving this next twenty-four hours means that I get to go home to my beloved bed."

The rest of the group echoed the sentiment. Radek offered everyone bottled water as Aya did her best to serve the evening meal in the random assortment of stoneware they'd managed to bring with them. They ate in relative good spirits, sharing stories about what they planned to do when they got out of the

Rapture. Everyone agreed that getting home to a hot shower, a proper meal and the cozy familiarity of their respective beds would be top of the list of things to do and never again take for granted. Topher wanted a burger. Connor wanted a hard drink. Radek offered to take first watch as Topher packed up the remnants of the meal.

Chloe asked if she could sleep inside the back seat of the truck. Aya agreed and Connor held on to the keys. Aya and Connor crawled into the bed of the truck and Topher into the lean-to. Radek selected a handgun and a better shotgun from the selection of weapons Aya and Connor had brought. Connor whispered to Aya in the bed and filled her in on what had happened with Topher.

"Are you hurt?" Aya asked immediately.

"Maybe just my pride," Connor replied, lying on his back and staring up at the blue of the tarp above them. "He's not stronger than I am, but he did get a lucky shot in with his knee to my gut." He ran his hand across his smooth stomach as he mentioned the sucker punch Topher had attempted to pull. "I wasn't expecting that."

"I'm sorry," Aya whispered.

"For what?"

"That you got into a fight."

"I'm used to fighting, been doing it all my life."

"Gotta admit I'm kinda flattered that you'd defend my honour like that."

Connor grinned. "I'm sorry that it happened at all. I didn't mean to sound..."

"No, I get it," Aya promised. "I really do appreciate it."

"I don't like it when people step into places they shouldn't be," Connor explained. "And I like it even less when my friends are liable to get caught in the crossfire when shit hits the fan."

"Do you think that he was telling the truth?"

"About what?"

"About everything?" Aya asked. "About being a former Controller? About Alphonse being insane enough to actually torture him in solitary imprisonment for a year?"

"I don't know," Connor replied slowly. "But, he did know things that lend a certain level of plausibility to his story."

"Like what?"

"He knew where the hordes were located in the other city," Connor pointed out. "Radek confirmed that he didn't even hesitate or make like he was guessing. He knew stuff about me. He knew stuff about Radek."

"How much do you think it could have been educated guesses, though?" Aya asked. "He knew what about you? That you're from Nottingham?"

"He knew I have a brother. He knew that he'd be pissed and probably calling in all sorts of favours from the IRA and God knows where else he's got favours to call in from."

"Isn't that a matter of public record?"

"IRA membership is definitely not a matter of public record," Connor said. "And I don't have a criminal record."

"So you believe his story?"

"I don't really see any reason not to believe his story."

"Don't trust him," Aya decided. "Not when things get hairy."

Connor agreed.

Aya sighed and rolled over onto her side, scooting a little closer to Connor as she shivered in the cool night air. "This is worse than I could have expected."

Connor grunted and rolled onto his side so he was facing Aya. He draped his arm across her waist but kept a modest distance between them. It was colder than he'd expected it to be and they'd given Chloe and Topher the only blankets they'd had, reasoning that there was two of them in a small space, it would be warmer than inside the truck or in the lean-to, even with a fire nearby.

"Don't fret," Connor said quietly. "You've got me. It'll be all right in the end."

"I wish I had half your optimism," Aya mumbled, her eyes half closed. "Maybe I wouldn't feel like giving up."

"You're not gonna give up," Connor whispered back. "I won't allow it."

Aya chuckled sleepily. "Can I give up and get some sleep?"

"I encourage that," Connor agreed. "I'll see you in the morning."

"Goodnight, Connor..." Aya mumbled as she drifted off to sleep. Connor moved closer to her, closing the space between them and Aya curled up, tucking herself against his chest to try and warm up. He didn't complain and eventually fell asleep to the sound of her breathing and the distant crackle of the fire.

They woke in the night to Topher shouting. Connor was up quicker than Aya and he rolled out of the bed, onto his knees in the back of the truck with his gun drawn as dark shapes materialized in the night. The camp had gone from idyllic and quiet, to a horror show in a matter of minutes as the field was quickly becoming overrun with shambling undead. The spell of peace was broken and the air was thick with the putrid smell of rotten, burning flesh.

"Goddammit!" Topher shouted, shooting at the oncoming horde. "These friends of yours, Connor?"

"Aw hell," Connor groaned as he pulled the tarp covering the bed of the truck down.

"Get in the truck, let's go!" He leapt over the tailgate and took aim, firing off several rounds into the closest of the zombies before running around to the driver's side door and unlocking it.

Aya steadied herself in the back of the bed, leaning against the tailgate and drawing her gun as Connor started the engine. "Radek!" she shouted.

Radek was shooting slowly, one round at a time with a careful pause between each shot. He'd been felling zombies with a slow and steady precision, but it wasn't enough. He'd be overrun and mowed down by sheer numbers if he didn't move.

"Radek, let's go!" Aya shouted again.

Dropping his gun to his side, he disappeared from the ring of firelight as he sprinted to the truck. Aya held her breath as she lost sight of him in the dark as the zombie horde stamped out the already dwindling fire. Radek appeared and climbed into the bed, landing hard on the mattress and huffing as he did. Aya kicked the back window, signalling Connor to get a move on.

"Topher, let's go, you idiot!" Radek shouted as Topher laughed with maniacal glee as he shot the oncoming half-burned zombies.

If he heard Radek, Topher made no indication of it. The zombies were approaching and he made no move to get into the truck. There were more zombies than he had bullets and Topher knew it. Finally, the shouting from Aya and Radek reached through the haze of exhaustion, fear, and bloodlust and spurred him to get a move on. He shot the closest zombie and then turned and sprinted as Connor started driving through the field. Radek reached out and grabbed Topher's hand as Aya took aim and fired at two zombies who were too close for comfort. It took Topher a moment of dangerously hanging from the back of the tailgate and barely balancing on the bumper as Connor drove through the darkened field before Radek was able to pull him into the truck. He landed harder on the mattress than Radek had and the sudden bump knocked Aya off balance, ruining her shot and nearly causing her to drop her gun. She growled her frustration and settled into the back of the truck as Connor picked up speed, heading toward City Two and away from the camp.

"So much for our camp out," Topher giggled. "I sure hope those bastards got some footage of that."

"Yeah," Aya agreed slowly, watching the horde of zombies diminish on the horizon as they made their way down the first of the big hills leading into City Two.

CHAPTER TWENTY

Ratings

Alphonse threw anything that he could get his hands on, papers, pens, clipboards, files, even someone's stray coffee mug. No one dared to speak while Alphonse was flying into a rage.

"Four hordes!" he screamed at no one in particular. "These bastards have destroyed four hordes and have run off into the middle of nowhere so we can't film them! Radek and Topher took a vehicle that had no recording equipment in it, and we lost Aya and Connor when the others picked them up!"

Alphonse continued his shouting, swearing a blue streak that made no sense.

Hilda stood at the back of the room, arms crossed, watching indifferently as her boss screamed until he was red in the face and panting. "Twelve hours," he muttered, finally.

"We've been without footage for more than twelve hours."

Hilda cleared her throat.

Alphonse looked over to her and ran a hand through his hair, slicking it back. He glared at her, his eyes glittering with malice as he carefully drew a handkerchief from his pocket and dabbed elegantly at the sweat beading on his forehead and neck.

"What?" he demanded.

Hilda shrugged and walked across the bullpen. She patted one of the technicians on the shoulder in a gesture of reassurance and solidarity. "We haven't been without footage," she pointed out. "Agent Seven has been a busy little bee, and every other camera has been endlessly scrolling through the footage."

Alphonse sneered. "So?"

"So," Hilda continued without missing a beat, "the cameras in the farmhouse where we'd dropped Aya? They ran until the fire she started melted them. We got footage of a horde of zombies burning to death. We got footage from the outdoor cameras of the barn burning. There's still a camera rolling on the burned out husk of the farm right now, it showed a few straggling zombies that managed to escape the wildfire shambling off to God knows where. The highway cameras? Running. We caught a bit of footage of Radek and Topher picking up Aya and Connor. We know they've banded together and were headed in the direction of City Two."

Alphonse grunted and shook his head. "Not enough."

"Are you kidding?" Hilda asked. "Have you seen the ratings?"

Alphonse stopped his moping. "No?"

"They're up tenfold. People who tuned out? They've come back. People who weren't watching before? Everyone has tuned in. The footage of the zombies in the fire? Most shared online. People are watching the videos, slowing them down, modifying them. There's conspiracy theorists popping up, saying that Aya knows exactly where everything is. There are people claiming she's in our pockets, that she's working with us. Most people are defending her, saying that we're the evil corporation and that everything we're doing is a public assassination attempt, and while they're not wrong, it's certainly fuelling the fire."

"What fire?"

"Online debates, mostly," Hilda replied with a shrug. "People are paying attention. There are protests happening everywhere right now, but no one is stepping in to stop this event. Everyone is waiting to see what we do next. If Aya makes it out alive, Alphonse, we are going to have to heighten security. If Aya dies, we're going to have a situation that we might not recover from."

"Has anyone figured out where we are yet?"

"Several people, but they've been silenced online already."

Alphonse ran his hand against his chin and mouth, thinking. "What about City Two?"

Hilda let out a mirthless chuckle. "I thought you'd never ask."

"Is it bad?"

"Define bad."

"Is the city on fire?"

"No," Hilda explained. "Agent Seven has been making demands almost nonstop, however."

"Demands like what?"

Hilda shook her head. "Nothing unreasonable. I think he's paranoid and afraid that we're going to change our minds about letting him get away with murder. He's taken the rest of the players hostage, Alphonse. He's set up traps around his base, wire traps, cans and jars on strings to make noise if a horde comes. He found the horde in the bowling alley, *and he left it alone.* He took the chocolate bars left in the concession and didn't touch a single zombie."

"Did we get that on film?"

"Yes," Hilda admitted. "And people want to know who the hell he is. No one can find any information on him and it's driving them into a frenzy. Your wild card has worked."

Alphonse nodded enthusiastically. "Excellent."

"Aya isn't our biggest problem, Alphonse. Agent Seven is killing his hostages."

"Let him."

Hilda's face paled. "Excuse me?"

"I'll be making an announcement shortly," Alphonse said. "We're releasing the rest of the hordes, and I want everything centred on City Two."

"You can't just release everything!" Hilda argued.

"There's no rules but my own," Alphonse argued. "I want you to release all the remaining zombies. I want all the backups to flood City Two. I want the highway leading back to City One cut off as soon as Aya's group gets down that damned hill into City Two. I want this to be a royal bloodbath. We have eight hours left. I want the ratings to skyrocket. To hell with security measures, make this happen."

No one in the Bullpen moved a muscle. Alphonse Ritter had gone insane.

"Did I stutter?" Alphonse shouted, spittle flying from his mouth.

Hilda clapped her hands twice, a sharp report echoing through the silent Bullpen. "You heard the man! Get to work! Dispatch the extra troops to release the zombies. Set up a roadblock on the highway. Someone get me eyes on Aya Wu and her group!"

"How many hostages does Agent Seven have left?" Alphonse asked suddenly.

"Unsure, sir," one of the technicians answered. "We're not quite sure. He killed two at least and carved them up as zombie bait, but we haven't seen anything else."

Alphonse frowned.

"Sir?" Hilda interrupted. "We have eyes on Aya's group. They're just entering City Two, they're driving past the bowling alley right now."

"Then get to work faster," Alphonse snapped. "I want the finale bloody, make it happen."

"You heard him!" Hilda shouted. "Make preparations, immediately."

Alphonse rubbed his hands together. "And get the PA system ready. I have an announcement to make."

CHAPTER TWENTY-ONE

Hilda

She tended to ask herself why she'd ever left her comfortable espionage job for dealing with Alphonse Ritter and his megalomania. Oftentimes when she asked herself this, she was knee-deep in gore and on the front lines to neutralize an attacking horde of zombies.

Or, she supposed, she asked herself the same question when she was the one assigned to collect the participants for the next edition of The Rapture.

Hilda wasn't even sure how Alphonse Ritter had managed to convince her to leave freelancing to work for him. They had met when she had taken a job to protect a "German-American businessman" going into a zombie-infested quarantine zone to assess damages and see what could be salvaged. She hadn't known that he was the man responsible for creating the Rapture. She hadn't known that Alphonse Ritter was not entirely sane when she'd agreed to protect him. She was good at what she did; killing zombies, extracting survivors from areas otherwise considered 'lost'. Before the dead began to rise, she had been a military officer, specializing in wet works and espionage. She didn't talk about her past very much, and anyone who asked her, regretted it.

Hilda sat quietly on the back of one of Alphonse's military trucks. She was covered in mud and blood and the scowl on her aquiline face was enough to keep anyone else away from her.

"What do you think?"

"I don't think that there's enough remains to bother sending home to anyone's families," Hilda drawled, spitting on the ground. "This was a bloodbath of the worst kind."

"What about the hordes?"

Hilda grunted. "They've mostly migrated to the north barricade. It won't be hard to destroy them there, or round them up if you'd prefer."

"Any positive ID's on any of the undead?" Alphonse asked.

"Of locals or of contestants?"

"Contestants."

"No. I'm pretty sure the contestants who weren't shot by other players were eaten by the horde," she informed her boss. "You do know that there have been things that go against most laws of America happening within these games, right?"

"I'm aware," Alphonse crooned. "But nothing is illegal during the Rapture, at least, not for the contestants."

"You didn't get a winner this year," Hilda pointed out. "Isn't that going to drive the protests up higher?"

Alphonse shrugged. "Let them protest all they want. It isn't going to change anything." A smile touched the corners of his mouth. "I think that I will make the winnings that didn't get claimed this year into a charitable donation. Perhaps we should call up Lila Wu, see where she'd prefer us to donate our money?" He laughed to himself and Hilda felt her blood run cold at the sound.

"Why do you let them bother you so much?" Hilda asked, finally. "They don't do anything worthwhile, they've not stopped you yet, and no one else has even come close to shutting you down."

"It's not that they bother me, Hilda, but would you let someone live in your house and criticize the way you cook every day?"

"This is not the same as an uninvited houseguest," Hilda pointed out. "You know that you could have them taken care of," she made a shooting motion with her fingers, "and all of your problems would be solved."

"I can't kill Lila and Aya Wu," Alphonse replied. "Are you kidding?"

"Killing the leaders of this little resistance would leave the others scattered and disorganized," Hilda pointed out. "There is no one else to take their place. The protests aren't strategic or military, Alphonse. They are a bunch of angry citizens who think your game is inhumane. There is nothing that they can do to you; they've proved to be useless already. Taking out the leaders would mean you have nothing to worry about. No more calls to politicians, no more bribing police. You could focus solely on your game."

Alphonse stared at Hilda.

Hilda shrugged. "Give me permission, I will go and fix your problem in ten minutes. They are planning another rally next week, and it would be an excellent time to take them out, especially because nobody won this year."

The look of cold calculation that crossed Alphonse Ritter's face in those moments gave Hilda pause, and not for the first time in her career. She felt suddenly ill at ease to be in the presence of this man. He was a machine, a shark beneath the face of a man who had overcome challenges unheard of before the dead began to rise. He was merciless and callous beneath the expensive suit and polished mannerisms. Hilda wondered, as she often did, if she had made a bigger mistake than she had realized when she'd agreed to work with him.

"No, Hilda, I think I have a better plan than an outright assassination."

"Have you?" Hilda asked, her voice cracking as her stomach clenched in fear and worry.

"Oh yes. Instead of turning them both into political martyrs, I think we shall have Aya Wu as our guest of honour."

"Guest?" Hilda echoed, afraid to hear exactly what her employer was thinking.

Alphonse nodded and clapped Hilda on the shoulder. "Yes, thank you for the idea, Hilda. Next year, we shall have Aya Wu participate in The Rapture as a contestant."

CHAPTER TWENTY-TWO

City Two

Connor stopped the car at the base of the hill where the land flattened out. The community centre of City Two was to their right. Aya sat at the very back of the bed, leaning against the window into the cab while Radek and Topher acted as lookouts. Connor idled the truck and got out, crossing over the back and leaning against the edge of the bed.

"Okay, we're here, Chloe is freaking out because this is where she says she came from and, according to her, there's a crazy son of a bitch who is turning the whole town into a giant booby trap."

"I'm inclined to believe her," Topher said, shooting nervous glances over at the community centre.

"No one asked you," Connor snapped. "But yeah, I see no reason to doubt her."

"Well, we can't exactly go back to the place where we started," Radek pointed out. "We sort of blew it up, and there's no food and no supplies to be found there, and we don't even know how safe it is anymore."

"If there was a third horde, and I'm pretty sure there would have been," Topher offered, "it would have been released by now."

Aya checked the cuff on her wrist. "Yeah, there's eight hours left. There should be one horde left to activate, I think?"

Their discussion was interrupted by the steady thrum of a helicopter flying overhead.

"What the hell?" Connor asked.

"They're getting rescue in position I guess?" Radek suggested

"That's not a rescue copter," Aya replied. "The rescue helicopters are red, medics are on board to make sure that there's no injuries and no one is infected. That's a military helicopter."

"What the hell are they sending military helicopters here for?"

"They have military helicopters at their disposal," Aya reminded Connor. "They've practically got their own private army."

"Well what the hell?"

Aya shrugged and looked to Topher and Radek for answers.

"Don't look at me," Radek replied with a smirk. "You're the expert around here."

Aya rubbed her temples in exhausted frustration. "We have just under eight hours," she said. "It's a twenty minute drive back to the other city, I just don't know that we've got enough gas? There's no guaranteed safety anywhere, and between this city and the other, there's a lot of open fields, and a few farms, but less houses than we'd hope."

"Not to mention that we have no idea how wide the playing field is," Connor pointed out. "For all we know, the barrier is half a field away and if we go just beyond the city, we're gonna hit the barricade, right?"

"Very true," Aya agreed with a nod.

"The barricade is literally a minute out of the other city," Radek offered. In any direction. We checked."

"Then we assume it's the same here," Aya said with a defeated sigh. "That means that this field is probably the end of the zone," she continued, pointing to just beyond the community centre. "That path is the old railroad tracks, beyond it is a thicket and some more farmland. Same thing is basically on the other side, and then it's a big hill. If you take the highway that we're on, it passes right down main street and then it's the big hill and it leads to another tow, which is probably where the Controllers have set up their base and where we'll go immediately after the game, assuming we survive."

The group was silent. They had no options, really. Another helicopter passed overhead and Aya watched it, frowning.

"They're doing something," Radek said. "I know it. They're changing something again."

"They have cameras on us again," Connor pointed out, gesturing toward the nearest light post. "See, that's one of theirs. They've probably not been to happy that we were out of range for as long as we were."

Aya looked up at the camera and she flashed a smile and waved at whoever was watching. "Well, I do hope that we get an announcement soon then."

"What do you want to do?" Connor asked. "You're the leader here, Aya."

"Lord help me," she muttered. "I don't want to make the wrong choice here."

Chloe knocked on the window to get everyone's attention. Aya scooted over so that she could open the back window. "Y'all are talking about what we're going to do, right?"

"Yeah, you got any input?" Aya asked.

"Well, I don't want to be here none," Chloe said. "But I also understand that we can't really go back the other way now can we?"

"What makes you say that?" Aya asked.

"I wouldn't want to go back the other way," Chloe said. "And with those helicopters circling overhead, I have a feeling that things aren't going to be going too well back that way."

"You said there's a guy here?"

"Took us all hostage. I ran the hell away, I don't know what he's done since I left but he isn't the kind of guy you want to mess with."

"We gotta take the chance here," Aya said.

Chloe nodded. "I know. That's why I'm not running. I know I'll be safer here with you than I was all drugged up and alone when he caught me."

Topher fidgeted nervously. "Have we made a decision then?"

"Yeah, we're going to find a place to hole up here," Connor sneered.

Aya nodded. Connor shot Topher another dirty look and climbed back into the truck. He drove slowly into the town, taking the first left to pass the gas station and stopped when they reached what was considered the main road.

Connor killed the engine and got out of the truck. Topher and Radek jumped out of the bed and walked around the front of the truck to see what Connor was swearing at. Aya stood up in the bed and climbed onto the truck's roof to see without being compromised.

The entire main road had been turned into an obstacle course. Cars had been moved into the road at odd angles, wires and ropes of jars and cans were strung up between the cars and the buildings, and barbed wire glinted in the early morning light. Sharpened broomsticks and picket fence pieces dotted the road, too, interspersed between trashcans and more wires.

"Those are traps, aren't they?" Radek said.

"They look like hunting traps, yeah," Connor agreed. "The cans and stuff are to make noise whenever something gets near. I'll wager he's holed up somewhere nearby."

"Try not to pay too much attention to the corpses," Aya pointed out from on top of the truck.

"Aw, fuck," Connor muttered, he hadn't even noticed the two bodies, still tied to a street lamp and an open car door.

Chloe heaved and threw up, opening the door and letting her stomach empty onto the pavement. Aya slid back down from her spot and hoisted her bug-out bag. She picked up Connor's bag, too and joined them, handing Connor his belongings.

"You still wanna go through here?" Connor asked, slipping his bag over his shoulders.

"We don't have much choice," Radek pointed out.

"We can go around," Aya said with a sigh. "There's houses that way," she pointed to their left. "If we follow the road, there's the rest of the town."

"I saw more traps that way," Radek said. "When I got out of the truck."

"We can go around the road then," Aya replied through gritted teeth. "Through the field."

"Let's just go through here," Radek argued. "It's quick and you can lead us away from here after we get through."

Before Aya could argue, Radek was already making his way through the booby traps, careful not to touch anything that would otherwise alert the man who had set them up. Aya shook her head.

"I'm not going through here," she complained.

Connor was about to argue when Radek shouted.

"Shit! I'm stuck!"

Connor instinctively moved forward to try and help, but Aya gripped his arm, holding him back. "No point in you getting stuck, too."

Connor growled. "What are you stuck on?'

"Barbed wire," Radek called back. "It was sticking out and caught my pants. I pulled this shit over and now it's a fucking mess."

Connor nodded. "Okay hang on," he said, setting his bag back down. "There's wire cutters in here somewhere from the shed you raided, Aya."

"Hey, guys?" Topher interrupted. "Don't look now, but we have company."

Aya nudged Connor and drew her gun as a whip thin man with sinewy arms and a grizzled face appeared from behind one of the buildings. He was dragging another person by a rope around their neck and pointing a sawed off shotgun at his hostage.

"Oh, look, I see we've caught some intruders," the scrawny man drawled. "What do you think you're doing here?"

"Look, man, we just want to get out of here," Connor said, holding his hands up. He was unarmed.

Aya's gun didn't waver and she kept the man approaching in her sights. "This your trap?"

"Yeah, and I see you've brought me some fresh meat to feed the zombies," he continued, jerking his head toward Radek. "I'll take him and whatever weapons you have, and the rest of you can go."

"I don't fucking think so," Connor snarled.

"You aren't in the position to negotiate," Agent Seven snapped back. "I have no intention of dying in the next eight hours, and you won't last if you don't do what I want, I'll make sure of it."

"Sorry, man, that's not my call to make," Connor argued. "Just let us go on our merry way and you can keep your hostages and whatever, no harm no foul."

Agent Seven's dark eyes darted over the group until they landed on the truck. A wicked smile lit up his whole face as he spied Chloe in the cab of the truck. "Ah, now, I think you do have something that belongs to me."

"And what's that?" Topher asked.

Agent Seven licked his lips and nodded toward the truck. "You've got my girlfriend in that truck of yours."

Connor looked back at the truck. "Oh, hell no."

"Then you can kiss your friend goodbye," Agent Seven replied, his gun moving to point at Radek. "You keep your friend, or you keep my girl, your choice."

"Or we shoot you," Topher suggested.

"Your little girl is shaking," Agent Seven pointed out. "And she's the only one of you with a gun." His twisted smile touched his face again, distorting it into a fun house parody of glee. "And look at who you've brought me. If it isn't Aya Wu," he licked his lips again, a slight shudder wracking his body at thoughts that were best left unspoken of. "Mm, now I think that I will trade all of you for her instead."

Connor stood, placing himself between Aya and Agent Seven. "Okay, this has gone on long enough," Connor barked. "Back off and let us take our friend out of your trap and we'll leave."

A sharp burst of static cut the air as the speaker system turned on. Alphonse's cold laugh filled the air. "Ah, good, I see you've met Agent Seven."

Aya handed her gun to Connor and he pointed it at Agent Seven, firming up the standoff as Alphonse's voice continued to drone on through the speakers.

"Now now, we can't have you all killing each other right now, can we? Alphonse asked with a chuckle. "That wouldn't do, and it would cut the last leg of the game drastically short, don't you think? No no, Agent Seven, lower your shotgun. These people aren't going to do anything to you, and yes, I assure you that your demands have been heard and they will be met, assuming you survive the final few hours and are picked up, uninfected by the rescue teams."

Agent Seven snorted and nodded his understanding but didn't lower his gun.

"As for the rest of you," Alphonse continued, "good show. You boring bastards have managed to destroy four hordes and not get killed. Bravo. I didn't think you'd make it this far, let alone team up and become an even bigger pain in my ass. I guess Aya's philosophy of peace and non-violence really does make everyone a better person when it gets right down to it."

Connor took a step back, forcing Aya to fall in closer behind him, and urging Topher to back off as well. Topher ignored him, staring intently at Agent Seven, his eyes darting over the booby traps before them, trying to figure out how to get Radek out without getting stuck himself.

"Well now, I suppose that since you've all decided to bend the rules and team up against me and my beautiful hordes, then it's only fair for me to announce that all bets are off. No more rules, no more time limits. No more rest. You have just under eight hours left? Well, I'm going to make these last eight hours the worst hours of your life. The road is blocked off. You're stuck here in this town. For eight hours. Hordes of zombies are on their way. You have only one mission now kiddos - survive, but for the love of God, make it interesting. Tick tock, children. See you in eight hours."

The PA system screeched one last time as it shut off and Alphonse's words hung bitter in the air.

CHAPTER TWENTY-THREE

Sacrifice

Agent Seven smiled maliciously. "Eight hours to survive?" he echoed. "Well then, I had best cut out this dead weight."

Aya screamed as the gun went off. The hostage collapsed to the ground, his head a bloody pulp that spattered noisily against the pavement. Topher retched but managed to not throw up. Radek closed his eyes and mouthed a silent prayer. Connor aimed his gun at Agent Seven, who wagged a finger.

"Don't pull that trigger, boyo," he taunted. "You hear that?"

Moans filled the air. Whatever hordes had been in stasis nearby had woken up to the sound of the gunshot.

"They can smell the blood!" Agent Seven crowed, laughing. "You had better make your choice! I know for sure there's a horde in the community centre you passed to get in here. I don't know where the rest are, but they'll be coming for you."

Connor's finger rested on the trigger for a lingering moment and he growled in frustration before lowering the gun. Agent Seven laughed and ran off, disappearing behind the restaurant that stood on the far corner.

"Fuck," Connor groaned.

"Come on," Topher said. "Give me the wire cutters, I'll get Radek out and then I know where we can go."

"You?" Connor repeated. "And why the fuck should we trust you?"

"Because I was on the team that designed this year's Rapture."

Aya nodded, her face set in a grim look of disgust. Connor had told her, but she didn't want to believe it until Topher said it himself. She slapped him in the face. "How fucking dare you," she growled. "How dare you treat us like friends and allies. You lied to us."

"I didn't lie," Topher argued, ignoring the stinging red welt on his face. "I told Connor."

"Fuck you," Aya snarled. "You knew all of this was happening. You knew..."

"I didn't know everything!" Topher snapped. "I knew where the hordes I had helped place were, and if I'm still right, then I know where we can go to at least regroup and be safe, but first off, we gotta get Radek out of that trap before the hordes come."

Aya growled and stormed back to the truck to tell Chloe about what was happening.

Connor shoved Topher. "Get Radek out of the trap, and take us to your safe house, you bastard."

Topher held out his hand for the wire cutters as the moaning and groaning of a horde got louder. Connor rummaged through his bug-out bag and handed Topher the wire cutters. Topher nodded and made his way through the maze the same way that Radek had, only more careful to avoid anything that could snag his legs and pants. He made it to Radek's side and crouched down, holding onto Radek's leg as he carefully cut the wire around him.

"You could have told me," Radek pointed out.

"If you were me, would you have said anything?" Topher asked.

"Probably not," Radek admitted. "I don't blame you."

"Well, I'm gonna make this right, I hope," Topher said. "Okay, you're free, lemme just pull this off your leg and we can go to my safe house."

Radek stood very still as Topher pulled the tangled wire out of his friend's pants.

"Fuck," Radek said, nearly losing his balance. "Horde up ahead."

Topher looked up. Radek was right. Spilling out of a ground level house down the block was a swarm of zombies. They were moving slower than normal, and Topher knew it was from the sedatives that the Controllers used to keep them under their control until it was time for the players to face them.

"Holy shit," Connor shouted. "Topher!"

"Yeah, I see them," Topher shouted back. "We gotta go around, though, the house is on the other side of the block!"

Connor fidgeted, trying to make up his mind. He dashed back to the truck where Aya and Chloe were waiting. "I have a plan. Stay in the truck, but be ready to get out and haul ass, okay?"

Aya nodded.

"Topher! Radek! Get in the truck!"

Topher tugged Radek's pants free, cutting his hands on the barbed wire in the process, but not saying anything. Radek pulled him to his feet and they hurried back through the maze of traps as the zombie horde fell upon the other side of the traps, clanking the bottles and cans together and howling as they were skewered by the pikes and cut by the wires as they tried to mindlessly force their way through. Topher shoved Radek into the truck and barely managed to close the door before Connor slammed on the gas. They went careening down the side road, Connor pushed the truck faster, closing the short distance between them and the other traps Agent Seven had set.

"Hold on!" Connor shouted as they crashed through the barricade on the other side. The truck's engine squealed and whined as Connor pushed it as far as it would go. He cleared them of as much of the debris as he could before the truck gave up. "Grab your shit!" Connor shouted. "Topher, lead us to your so-called safe house."

Aya grabbed her bug-out bag and helped Chloe from the car. Chloe landed hard on her leg and nearly toppled but Aya caught her. "Topher, hurry your lying ass up!" Aya shouted.

Topher had his crossbow out and a gun slung over his shoulder. "This way!"

Radek and Connor stood defensively behind Aya as she helped Chloe to move forward. A groan sounded and it chilled Aya to the bone. Everything stopped for a heartbeat as zombies appeared from around the corner.

"Holy shit, run!" Connor shouted, waving his hand, shooing Aya and Chloe.

"This way," Topher yelled, reaching out for Aya.

Aya followed Topher, shooting constant looks over her shoulder as Connor and Radek stood their ground, walking slowly backward and shooting any zombie that got too close.

"The traps are slowing them down, just go!" Connor yelled at Aya. "We'll be right behind you."

Aya did as she was told and helped Chloe move as fast as she could behind Topher.

"Oh God," Chloe muttered, pointing.

Aya looked to where she was pointing. There were more zombies spilling from a small house on the very edge of the boundaries of the town. Aya swore a streak in Mandarin.

"Connor!"

Connor turned to look at why Aya was shouting. "Oh, mother*fucker* are you kidding me?" He turned away from Radek; the zombies coming around the corner weren't the biggest threat as they were greatly slowed by the truck and the debris from the traps. He opened fire into the oncoming horde that had appeared, picking off three of the closest ones with three well-executed shots. Gray matter and blood sprayed before the zombies fell forward, hitting the ground with wet thuds and twitching as their nervous systems shut down for the last time.

"Radek!" Connor shouted. "Come on, man, we gotta get a move on."

Radek grunted and hurried to catch up with Connor. They moved as quickly as they could, keeping an eye out for approaching zombies. Gunshots filled the air as they held off the oncoming horde and followed behind Topher.

Topher led them to a house on the very edge of town, overlooking a short drop to a field below. It was too far to jump down and the drop was mostly straight with a few jutting rocks. Not the most ideal place, but it had certainly been overlooked. He pulled a key out of his pocket and unlocked the door.

"In here!" he shouted. There were a few steps leading up to the front door, not the most effective way to stop a zombie attack, but it was better than nothing, and there weren't huge picture windows in the front room. Aya and Chloe followed and Topher stood at the front door until Radek and Connor were both safely inside.

Aya threw her arms around Connor as soon as he was inside the house. "Are you hurt?"

Connor shook his head. "No, we're okay, right Radek?'

Radek was leaning against the wall, doubled over, catching his breath and trying not to throw up. He gave Connor a weak thumbs up.

"Yeah, see?" Connor said with a wry smirk. "We're all good."

"All right, you filthy fucking traitor," Aya said, wheeling on Topher. "What the hell is this place?"

"You're welcome for saving your sorry asses," Topher replied with a snarl. "Welcome to the safe house. It's a complete dead zone. No cameras, no bugging equipment, nothing. There's food stocked in the pantry and there should be coffee. There's a radio, too."

"Nothing works, you know that," Aya pointed out.

"Yeah, but this is a satellite radio," Topher replied. "And I worked on prepping this game, remember? I was kicked off the team for protesting your involvement and I was thrown in prison for a year. This was set up almost three years ago. You've been target one for a long time. You weren't supposed to make it this far. The fact that I'm still here, too, means that Alphonse is losing control of everything and he's going to stop at nothing to make sure that he wins this round. The extra zombies? They were failsafes in case you made it this far. I planned this house as a total dead zone, I fudged the system when I was installing cameras and microphones and I specifically overlooked this house. The radio will work, feel free to make a call if you want to."

Aya looked at Connor. "You've got someone to call, haven't you?" she suggested.

Connor nodded slowly. "Yeah. I do. Excuse me."

Aya stared at Topher and slowly shook her head. "You're an asshole."

"I know, I'm sorry."

"Thank you," Aya said, holding out her hand.

Topher took it and they shook, solidifying their truce.

Aya glanced around the house at the scared, exhausted friends she'd made so far. "What do you guys think? Food?"

--

"Where the fuck did they disappear to now?" Alphonse shouted, slamming his hands on the control panel. "Get me visual on Aya and her group!"

The technician did as he was told, flipping through camera views and showing different angles of town as zombies meandered their way through the empty streets. Agent seven showed up on several shots, fighting off zombies and running back and forth between his base and the streets, picking off the horde as much as he could while building new traps for the undead monsters to get stuck in. So far, he hadn't sacrificed any more of his hostages, but Alphonse knew that it was only a matter of time.

"S-sorry, sir," the technician stammered. "Aya and her group don't seem to be anywhere within sight of the cameras."

"Get the cameras in the houses up and running, then," Alphonse snapped. "I want eyes on every inch of this town until the end of the game. This has gone on long enough and I need to know where Aya Wu is at all times. She cannot be allowed to escape the Rapture."

The technician made a bit of a whimpering noise as he followed his orders. More monitors flickered to life as the shift of technicians changed.

"Find me Aya Wu!" Alphonse shouted at the new shift. "I don't care what it takes, you find her and then figure out a way to get her back on the playing field!"

Hilda walked down the steps from the catwalk where she had been watching Alphonse have his breakdown. Her boss hadn't slept much in the three days that the Rapture was happening, and she knew he wouldn't get a proper sleep until the whole thing was over. She calmly approached him and gave him a cup of coffee.

"Herr Ritter," Hilda crooned. "Have a cup of coffee and relax. All is not lost."

Alphonse took the coffee and scowled at Hilda. "What makes you say that?"

Hilda pointed to one of the screen that showed Agent Seven shooting zombies. "Your wild card is still in play."

A slow, deranged smile crossed Alphonse's face. He shoved the technician he had been yelling at out of the way, rolling the helpless techie's chair across the floor of the Bullpen. He pressed the buttons to turn on only part of the PA system and leaned in to the microphone.

"Hello Agent Seven. I have a proposition to make you."

On the screen, Agent Seven looked up at the camera from where he was building a new trap for the zombies. "I'm listening," he said.

"Find me Aya Wu, get her back on the playing field. I'll triple your reward. If you win, by yourself with no other survivors? I'll double the amount that I've already offered to triple. I'll give you six times the winnings, plus the fee you were promised, plus immunity for your crimes and I will personally move you into a tropical mansion paradise."

Agent Seven's face split into a wide grin, his crooked teeth glinting in the light of the street lamp. He gave a thumbs up to the camera and left his half-finished trap.

Alphonse looked at Hilda, who had gone pale. "Thank you for reminding me of my wild card."

--

Connor joined the group in the kitchen after his call. Topher was pulling food out of the pantry and Aya was cooking. Radek was tending to Chloe's injured leg, wrapping it with ace bandages to steady it and giving her painkillers. Everyone was joking, and the house smelled of coffee and cooking food. Connor helped himself to a cup of coffee and drank it black. He leaned against the counter and watched Aya finish preparing the meal.

"What've you got cooking?" he asked.

"Instant rice and a couple of random canned things all mushed together to make a sort of vegetarian chill?" Aya suggested, like she wasn't quite sure what she'd made.

"Sounds good."

"You make the phone call?"

Connor nodded. "Coordinates are traced, but it's not like they didn't know where we are. Apparently the internet has taken quite a shine to us. People will be here in a few hours, hopefully to see me to the winner's circle."

Aya nodded. "I'm getting us the fuck out of here."

Connor grinned. "How much coffee did you drink already?"

"Three cups, and I didn't skimp on the condensed milk and sugar."

"There's condensed milk?" Connor asked. "And I'm drinking this shit black?"

Aya laughed and handed over the can of milk. Connor fixed his coffee and sipped at the sweet mixture, a look of bliss on his face. "Much better."

"Good," Aya replied with a nod. "You can help me serve dinner."

The chatter didn't stop over dinner. It was the first time that they had felt truly at ease since they'd been thrown into the Rapture. Connor fidgeted with the bug out bags, taking food out, since they wouldn't need it now. He handed Aya a knife and instructed her to stick it in her boot. Aya did as he said and readjusted the laces to make it more comfortable. Connor handed guns and ammunition out to the others, letting everyone pick a gun they were comfortable with.

"No more chances," Connor said firmly.

Their jovial mood turned sour when the roar of a truck engine filled the house. It was close, and getting louder. Everyone was up in a heartbeat, but they barely had time to register what was going on before the truck they heard smashed through the front wall of the house. Chloe screamed as the front wall collapsed around the truck. Connor swore as Topher and Aya coughed dust. They didn't have long to recover from the shock as the air was soon filled with the sounds of zombies.

"What the hell?" Connor demanded.

The truck pulled back slowly, reversing from the hole it had made. Through no small miracle, the truck was still able to run. As the dust settled, the truck's lights turned on, blinding the group inside. Zombies began to shuffle through the hole in the wall, climbing over one another to get to the warm humans inside. Agent

Seven was sitting in the cab of the truck, grinning like a madman, despite the blood running down his face from a cut he'd sustained in the crash.

Connor opened fire on the truck, aiming for Agent Seven, but with no luck. The zombies were making their way into the house and Connor growled his frustration before changing targets and shooting the undead.

Aya grabbed her bag. "Upstairs! Go!" she shouted, shooting a zombie but missing its head. "Fuck," she snarled, shooting a second time and felling her target.

Chloe was limping; the bandages around her knee where Agent Seven had struck her were making it harder for her to move quickly. Topher offered her his back, lifting her easily and heading for the stairs. Aya moved to follow.

Connor swung the butt of his rifle into the head of a zombie that and gotten too close, crushing its skull and hammering the rest of its head into a fine paste in the carpet when the first Molotov cocktail hit the floor. Connor kicked the burning bottle away from him, but it rolled, dripping gasoline and igniting the carpet. He shot a wild-eyed look at Agent Seven. He was standing on the roof of his truck, lighting another.

"You son of a bitch," Connor snarled, raising his gun once more to take aim at the madman.

Radek yelped, drawing all attention to him. A zombie had grabbed him and sunk its teeth into his arm.

"No!" Aya shouted.

"Fuck!" Connor echoed.

Agent Seven cackled gleefully from his place on the roof of his truck, holding another Molotov cocktail and watching the confusion inside.

"Go," Radek begged, shoving the zombie away and killing it with a single shot. "Go. I'll cover you." He flashed Aya a soft smile. "It is my honour to die protecting you, Aya Wu. Thank you for a lovely dinner."

Tears fell freely down Aya's face from where she stood halfway up the stairs. Radek smiled back and nodded before turning and walking into the middle of the oncoming zombies. He shot the closest ones and began swinging his rifle when he ran out of ammunition. Connor took the chance to bolt, grabbing Aya around the waist and dragging her up the stairs as Radek's screams mingled the with crackling of the catching flames and the guttural grunting of the zombies as they ate him.

"This way!" Topher yelled. "To the roof!"

Connor dragged Aya with him as he followed Topher. They clambered through the attic space and out onto the sloping roof, one after another as flames began to leap up the walls.

"Great," Chloe sneered. "Now we're stuck on a roof."

Topher shook his head and pulled a ladder through the crawlspace. It was a wide metal one and he hoisted it proudly. "Not quite."

Connor nodded approvingly. "Good, we can climb across the rooftops, but we're fucked as long as that crazy son of a bitch is down there."

"We'll deal with him next," Topher said. "First, let's get away from the fire."

Connor nodded and let Topher do the honours of setting up the ladder and helping Chloe across. Connor had more pressing things to worry about. Aya was sitting quietly, unmoving, while tears poured down her cheeks.

"Come on, Aya. You gotta move," Connor said quietly. "Burning to death isn't how Radek would have wanted you to go."

Aya nodded after a long moment and allowed Connor to help her cross the roof.

CHAPTER TWENTY-FOUR

IRA

As soon as Connor had gone missing, Mac had called in as many favours as he could. Connor wasn't the kind of person to just get up and disappear. He would have told Mac he was going away, at the very least. The brothers had taken several sabbaticals over the course of their tenure in the Army, and the sabbaticals had gotten a little more frequent since the undead had become a dominant force in the world. But they always told each other vaguely where they were going, just in case something happened, and they were never without contact for longer than a few hours, they always checked in when they got where they were going.

Mac was in a panic. He was barely functioning, not eating, not sleeping. He'd been calling Connor's cell phone every half hour for almost a day and a half, with no answer and no voicemail. Something wasn't right and Mac had no idea what it was. Connor didn't just run away. No one had heard from him, and there was no reason for Connor to be on a silent mission for the Army. Mac would have known about that, at least. Neither of the brothers worked without the other unless is was absolutely necessary, and even then, they'd always managed to negotiate terms to work together to avoid things happening to one or the other. They worked best as a team and everyone knew it. There was no reason for one to be gone without the other. It unnerved them, and Connor wasn't exactly the stronger of the two when it came right down to it.

Mac had managed to get himself dressed and presentable and leave the apartment. He knew he needed to eat something, and the thought of going outside to get some fresh air staved off the worry and panic he felt over Connor's sudden disappearance. He knew in his guts that this wasn't the IRA's doing. He knew that he and Connor were on good terms with their bosses, even though Connor had asked for a discharge. Had the Army decided that Connor was a liability, they would have had to tell Mac. There was no other way to keep the brothers on good terms. Mac knew it wasn't what he was fearing, there had to be another explanation but he wasn't seeing it. He made his way out of the gated community and back into the city proper.

Everything was in relatively easy walking distance and the fresh air was helping to calm Mac's frayed nerves. He had ordered himself take out, and had stopped for a latte from Starbucks. He was passing an electronics store with live television broadcasting in the windows, displaying the newest and most advanced televisions available on the market. Mac usually ignored the flashing propaganda, but today, he stopped to watch the flashing lights and quick cuts meant to distract and enthral. And then, the year's Rapture contestants were announced and everything clicked into place.

--

"Son of a bitch, son of a *bitch*." Mac hadn't turned off the television since the beginning of the Rapture. He'd been making calls and checking internet records, anything he could do to try and figure out where Connor had been taken, he was doing. Half the active members of the IRA were in Mac's pocket, and if they weren't in Mac's pocket, they owed Connor. Even their leader had reached out to the community to see if anyone had any information that could help them locate the current battlefield of the Rapture. Mac was sitting in front of his computer, scrolling through the endless social media feeds, with a separate window open for forums arguing about the human rights issues stemming from the removal of all announcements within the structure of the Rapture, and whether the Controllers were violating various by-laws that had been implemented when the Rapture was first approved by no longer making announcements for the benefit of the players.

Mac didn't really care. He was of the opinion that not making announcements meant that the Controllers in charge of the Rapture couldn't taunt the players, and overall, it was probably better for everyone's mental health. But what did he know? He wasn't a human rights activist; he was a hired gun who had done his fair share of less than decent things in the name of a job, and in the name of loyalty to Connor, and to their employer.

There were a few places in the forums that had made some progress in identifying the location of the current Rapture, but so far, no one had made any kind of solid argument for where they were fighting. Anything that got too close would be taken down by the Controllers, and Mac was starting to despair.

He reached for the bottle of whiskey next to his computer and took a long pull without pouring it into a glass. He swivelled his chair away from the computer screen to face the TV, and slouched forward, bottle dangling loosely in his hand as he rested his elbows on his legs. His face was pallid and the dark circles under his eyes betrayed exactly how little he'd slept in the time that Connor had gone missing. He had spent even more of his time fretting over Connor's well being and swearing at the television whenever Connor wasn't visible on the feed.

So far, Mac knew that Connor was still alive, even though he wasn't being picked up by any of the feeds. Further, the deaths were always displayed prominently when they occurred and the ticker tape at the bottom would run an 'in memoriam' piece once every hour. Luckily, Connor's name hadn't come up yet.

"And yet again, you've gone and fucked off, haven't you?" Mac muttered to the television. "How do you keep managing to get into spaces where there aren't any goddamn cameras, Conn?" He glared at the television, squinting into the split screen feeds, hoping to catch a glimpse of his brother. He'd lost sight of him as he'd driven the truck he'd been using through a barricade. Mac had held his breath, silently praying, as he watched his brother shooting an oncoming horde of zombies. He hadn't been able to appraise his brother, to check for injuries, but from the way that Connor was walking, and the way his hand trembled ever so slightly when he drew his gun to shoot the oncoming zombies after crashing the truck; Mac knew he was starting to fray around the edges.

"Dumbass probably hasn't slept," Mac muttered, taking another pull from the bottle. "Not like I can say much about that..." Mac settled into comfortable despair, his shoulders slumping in exhaustion and worry, barely able to keep his eyes open as the television feeds switched yet again, showing a replay of the burning farmhouse and Connor disappearing into the night. It had been the thing that kept him up, the thought of losing Connor to a zombie horde, and then watching him burn a house down to protect himself and that girl... It was the things that Mac's nightmares were made of. He saw the image of the zombies burning every time he closed his eyes, and the zombies always looked like Connor.

Mac's head snapped back and he forced himself to sit up. He'd almost dozed off. He coughed and gripped the whiskey tighter, setting it back on the desk, since he was liable to drop it if he fell asleep. He groaned to himself and ran tired hands over his face, digging the heels of his hands into his eyes. He was at the point where giving up seemed like a better idea than scouring the internet for clues about his brother's whereabouts. There were eight hours left in the game, and so far, Connor had managed to survive. The likelihood of him getting killed now was increased as there were more hordes of zombies supposedly being released into the small town, and while he'd managed to convince the majority of the survivors to team up with him, Mac supposed that Connor had a better chance of surviving the whole thing as long as he didn't do something stupid and heroic in the last few hours of the game. People were irrational under huge amounts of stress, and Mac knew better than anyone that Connor was just as irrational as the rest of the world, but he tended to sway toward the heroic, which was just as foolish as snap decisions involving violence to meet an end.

"You better not be dying from an avoidable zombie bite, Conn," Mac muttered to himself as he turned his chair back to face the computer. Nothing new had cropped up. It was still a bunch of useless drivel. Back and forth banter about human rights and a betting pool on who was going to die next. Mac felt his stomach clench at the callousness of some of the people on the forums. His fingers hovered over his keyboard as he tried to gather his thoughts well enough to argue with the assholes online. He hesitated, casting a longing glance at the bottle of whiskey close at hand, and then back to the posts flashing on the computer screen in front of him. He moved his hands away from the keyboard and folded them in his lap, content to watch and not engage. He already had his people looking for him. He didn't need to get more involved than he already was. There would be time to act when people called him with their findings.

As if willed into existence from Mac's self-control at not engaging online antagonists, his cell phone rang shrilly in the quiet of the room. Mac's heart skipped a beat as he reached for the phone. Someone had come through for him.

"Hello?" Mac asked desperation colouring his voice. "Please tell me you have good news."

"Mac?"

Mac's heart leapt into his throat. No way it was him, there was no way he wasn't dreaming. It took him a moment before he could regain his voice and ask. "Conn? Issat you?"

"Oh thank God, this thing is fucking working," Connor breathed, his voice heavy with relief of the other end of the phone. "Don't start cryin' Mac. I got work for you to do."

Mac grinned to himself and pinched the bridge of his nose, willing away the tears that had filled his eyes at the sound of his brother's voice. "Good fuckin' job there getting picked up for the God damn Rapture, Conn."

"Yeah, I'm just the luckiest son of a bitch this side of Nottingham."

"How did you even manage to call?"

"One of the guys here used to work for the Controllers. He somehow managed to set up a safe house for this particular game. I dunno how, but he did it. He blocked all the jammers and essentially made this a dead zone to the Controllers, so I'm on a satellite phone of some kind, and we have food and if we can relax here for the next couple of hours, we should be able to get out all in one piece."

"You hurt?" Mac asked.

"Not really. Achy. Tired. To be expected in this kind of situation though, right?"

"Not bit?"

"Not bit. I'm getting the hell out of this Mac, don't you worry, but I need your help."

"I've already got people on this," Mac said slowly. "Tell me what you need."

"So there's a girl," Connor started.

Mac laughed audibly, the sheer insanity of Connor talking about a girl in the middle of a kill or be killed game show was just what Mac needed to push him over the edge into exhausted giddiness. "How can you think about that when you're halfway to being eaten?"

"You know Aya Wu?"

"That protestor who finally got scooped up to prove a point."

"Yeah, her."

"She as cute in person as she on TV?"

"Yeah."

Mac grinned to himself. "Okay, she wants this thing taken apart as much as anyone, right?"

"Yeah, but we can't do it from where we are right now."

"Okay..."

"And I'm not telling anyone about this. The less people who know what's going on, the better. I can't let the others know that I have you working on this. I can't risk them getting sloppy. I need everyone to believe that we're just gonna get out of here ourselves, y'know?"

"I get it," Mac replied. It was underhanded, but he understood why Connor wouldn't tell the others. There was no guarantee that the IRA would even allow Connor to help the others when all was said and done. And there was still no guarantee that everyone would be getting out alive to start with. This was the stupid kind of heroism bullshit that Mac had hoped Connor would be able to avoid. Mac guessed that it would have been a miracle if Connor hadn't managed to figure out some kind of heroic bullshit to pull. "Do you have a plan?"

"Kind of?" Connor hesitated. "I need people to infiltrate the military thing the Controllers have set up. You're gonna have to come get us from the winner's ceremony. And if it goes like it has in the past," he continued, his voice taking on a devious tone that Mac knew too well, "we're going to have some very unpleasant words with a certain Grand Controller, if you know what I'm saying."

Mac nodded even though Connor couldn't see it. It was risky as hell and Mac wasn't entirely sure that he could even pull it off, but he was sure as hell going to try. "So you want us to come get you?"

"How many members can you get up here in the next eight hours?"

"I have at least a dozen ready to go," Mac said, grabbing a pad of paper and a pen. "Maybe more. Tell me what you need us to do for real and I'll get things going."

"Thank you, Mac," Connor said. "I owe you big time."

"Just don't die before we can come and rescue your ass," Mac replied.

"Promise that you'll get Aya outta here at least?" Connor asked. "If we make it... If she makes it and I don't... she's gonna be a target no matter which way this goes in the end."

"I promise," Mac replied. "You have my word that I'll make sure she's safe. So... Where are you?"

The smile in Connor's voice was unmistakable as he took a breath to explain where he thought that he was located. "You're not going to believe it."

CHAPTER TWENTY-FIVE

Final Showdown

They zigzagged their way across rooftops, staying as low as they could and trying to keep an eye out for Agent Seven. He was driving through the hordes of zombies below, methodically setting fires with his gasoline Molotov cocktails, between mowing down patches of the undead. Every now and again, the group could hear him laughing maniacally as he lit a group of zombies on fire.

"Where are the rest of the hostages?" Connor wondered after the third fire started.

Topher nudged Connor and pointed to a side street where a group of zombies had dog piled on top of themselves, eating something. Connor shuddered.

"It's how he's getting around," Topher pointed out with a shrug. "It's a pretty good plan, unfortunately."

"Yeah," Connor agreed. "So is lighting half the town on fire to smoke us out."

"He can't burn every house down, he'd be screwed too."

"We've got like two hours left," Connor pointed out. "He probably doesn't care. As long as he's in that truck, he's pretty much unstoppable."

"So we have to get him out of the truck," Chloe interrupted.

"Pretty much," Connor agreed.

"Fuck," Topher muttered. "How do you expect us to be able to do that?"

Connor shook his head. "I don't know."

Topher shot a look over at Aya, who was laying on her back near the edge of the roof, not moving, staring at the lightening sky. "Is she catatonic?"

Connor stole a glance at Aya. "I don't know," he admitted. "She's taking Radek's death to heart."

"We all are," Chloe said. "Poor girl, she's not meant for this."

"This was meant to kill her," Connor pointed out. "She was never meant to make it this far. The first horde of zombies we found, it was in her childhood home. She knows this area; it's where she grew up. We burned down the last safe place she'd ever known. I think she's handling this pretty well, all things considered."

"I can hear you," Aya announced. "I'm okay. I think. Mostly." She sat up and turned to face her friends. "I really just needed a few minutes to think."

Connor and Topher exchanged worried glances. Aya was looking haggard and pale, with dark circles under her eyes. She looked like she'd aged in the last few hours, that all the stress they'd been under just latched on to her and Radek's sacrifice pushed her over the edge.

"We need a plan," Connor said finally.

"We need to get Agent Seven out of that truck," Topher replied. "And we need to figure out where the hell we can hide out for the last hour."

"He's burning the city," Chloe said again. "He's trying to drive us out."

Aya frowned and tapped her chin, thinking. "It's me they want," she said slowly. "I'm the reason you're all getting screwed into this."

"You're not sacrificing yourself," Topher interrupted. "I won't let you."

"Why not?" Aya asked. "This was all a set up to kill me."

"Not anymore. Fuck that."

"We all want piece of that maniac down there," Chloe added. "So don't you go thinking about letting yourself die in the name of some misplaced sense of duty."

Aya nodded and pursed her lips. "I don't know, then."

Connor pointed. "What's that tall building there?"

Aya looked over to where Connor was pointing. She eyed the familiar blue, rectangular building and frowned. "That's the hotel," she said. "It's right on main street. There's a bar on the main floor, probably still stocked with booze."

"You think here's zombies inside?" Connor asked.

"When I was working on this project, we had considered putting a horde in the bar," Topher said. "I don't know if that was ever done, but there's likely a few on each floor, just in case anyone decided that they wanted to hole up there for the duration of the game."

"Anything useful stashed away in any of the rooms?" Connor asked.

Topher shook his head.

"We head there," Connor said. "Hole up on the roof."

"I'm going to lure out Agent Seven," Topher said. "You guys go ahead, I'll go to the ground, call him out. You snipe him from the roof."

"I'll lure him out," Chloe interrupted. Let me. I can't shoot a gun to save my life. My aim is terrible and he'll be more inclined to chase me through the alleys than you. You go into the hotel and let me in."

"You're injured," Topher argued.

"I'm all right," Chloe argued back. "I want a piece of the son of a bitch as much as the rest of you do. He's the one who hobbled me. He was going to leave me out as bait for the zombies just like the rest of them. You guys have done nothing but protect me and feed me. You've made sure I got this far; I can't just sit on the sidelines and cry. I have to pull my own weight in this thing. You're not arguing me out of this, Topher. As much as I appreciate you looking out for me like this, I'm making up my mind and I'm going to act as bait. He wants me back, he's got whatever sick little scenario it is that gets his rocks off playing in his head and I guarantee that he's not gonna back down from getting another crack at feeding me to the zombies."

"You don't have to do this," Connor offered. "The fact that you're injured..."

"Means that in the grand scheme of things I'm a hindrance," Chloe interrupted. She offered Connor a small smile. "No, you guys have done more than enough for me. Let me go and act as bait. If I die here, at least I've made up for running away and letting those other hostages die."

"There's no arguing you out of this is there?" Topher asked. "Chivalry and all that, y'know."

Chloe chuckled under her breath. "No, there's no talking me out of this."

Topher sighed and nodded. "Thought as much. Then, we'll both go."

"I'll let you into the hotel," Aya offered. "I'll break in on one of the upper floors, make my way to the main floor and unlock the doors. We'll leave Connor on the roof, to take Agent Seven out, since he's a sniper."

There was a moment of silent contemplation as everyone thought the plan through. It wasn't perfect by any means, but it was really the only plan that anyone could come up with. They all knew that Agent Seven was their biggest problem, and that until someone could kill him, or at the very least, get him out into the open, they were screwed. As long as the rest of their group stayed on the rooftops, they would be okay. Zombies weren't as big of a problem as Agent Seven and his chaotic insanity.

"I'm okay with this plan," Topher agreed.

"All right," Chloe said. "Let's do this."

Connor and Aya made their way across the rooftops, crawling across the ladder as Topher and Chloe hit the streets running. There was a fire escape on the back of the hotel and

Connor placed the ladder against it, holding it steady for Aya as she climbed up. He followed as fast as he could and they made it to the roof without incident.

Aya grabbed Connor and kissed him quickly. "Don't get killed," she asked him.

"Same for you," he replied.

Aya snorted a laugh. "Good luck," she added before climbing back down the fire escape and kicking open the first window she could find.

Connor settled himself on the rooftop, getting his rifle ready.

Chloe ran out into the open and began shouting. Topher ran to the other side of the street and started throwing trashcans. Agent Seven's truck appeared from around the corner. His engine revved as he debated on who to chase first.

Chloe broke first, taking off at hobbled sprint. Agent Seven followed.

"Fuck!" Topher shouted. Chloe had gone the wrong way to get Agent Seven into sniping distance.

--

Inside the hotel was dusty and dingy and Aya frowned. Things had really gone to hell, and part of her wondered how long the towns had been abandoned before the Rapture, or if it had always been this much a dive inside the hotel. Shaking her head to clear out the idle thoughts, she hurried down the stairs but stopped short as she reached the main hall that opened up into the front reception and the bar. The unmistakable grunting and groaning of zombies on the other side of the door had her blood running cold. She turned and sprinted up the stairs, back to the third floor where she'd come in. She stopped in the doorway of the stairwell and nearly cried out in her despair. There were zombies in the rooms and her running had woken them up.

"Fuck," she whispered, drawing her handgun. She needed to get to the fire escape and back to the roof. If there were zombies on this floor, there would be zombies everywhere else. There was no way she was getting to the main floor to let anyone into the hotel. Not without backup and more guns. Their plan had just fallen apart at the seams. With shaking hands, she took aim at the shambling bodies filling the hallway. There weren't many zombies, yet, but Aya had no way of knowing how many more there were, and she didn't entirely trust herself to kill them all without waking up the rest that were, she assumed, lingering in stasis or unaware of the presence of a living, breathing human. Her eyes darted around the hallway, counting the zombies shuffling out of the rooms and into the hall.

There weren't as many as she'd thought, but there were too many for her liking. Maybe, she decided, she could trap some of them in the rooms if she had a melee weapon. Her eyes fell on the emergency axe by the stairs and she sent a silent prayer of thanks to any god that might be listening. She just hoped that she wasn't being a complete idiot.

--

Chloe hobbled as fast as she could down an alley. Agent Seven was close behind her. She turned a corner, thinking it was a way out and she tripped over her own feet as she tried to stop. She'd run right into the horde of zombies that had been devouring one of Agent Seven's sacrifices. Chloe whimpered and turned to run back the other way but Agent Seven pulled in, blocking her. Chloe was shaking. She raised her gun and took two shots at the truck. The windshield splintered and cracked but the bullets didn't go through. Tears poured down Chloe's face, she knew she was trapped. She turned to face the horde, shooting as many zombies as she could as they fell upon her, teeth gnashing and arms outstretched.

Her screams echoed across the city.

Chloe's death was televised and the outcry was instantaneous.

Agent Seven backed his truck slowly out of the alley, in search of Topher.

Connor swore and raged on the roof. He could hear Chloe screaming and there was nothing he could do about it. Topher appeared on main street.

"Connor?" he called.

Connor poked his head over the edge of the roof. He waved and held a finger to his lips. Topher fidgeted nervously and ran up to the front door of the hotel. He was about to pull it open when he noticed shapes moving behind the glass. His heart plummeted as he heard the groaning coming from within.

"Shit!" he shouted. "Connor! There's zombies in the hotel!"

Connor's head appeared over the edge of the roof again. "What?"

"Inside!"

"Aya's in there!" Connor's voice rose in fear as gunshots echoed inside the hotel. "Shit!"

"Go get her! I'll get Agent Seven."

Connor dropped the rifle off the side of the hotel and Topher caught it easily. "Go!"

Connor nodded and disappeared; clambering down the fire escape, gun in hand.

Topher balanced the gun as he stood on the step of the hotel. Agent Seven's truck appeared by the restaurant across the street. Agent Seven climbed out of the truck and Topher took aim. Agent Seven hadn't seen him.

Topher placed his finger on the trigger, and the door behind him shook, jolting him and making him miss his shot. The wooden door splintered behind him and undead hands reached through the broken wood.

"Holy shit!"

Rotting, bloodied hands grabbed at Topher and he screamed wordlessly, pulling away. He took aim at Agent Seven. Agent Seven reached into his truck and pulled out his own gun. Topher stumbled forward, pulling away from the hands reaching out to tear at his flesh, stumbling down the steps as Agent Seven's first shot buried itself in the wood of the door where Topher had been standing moments ago.

"Rot in hell!" Topher shouted as another two shots whizzed past him, missing. He held his breath and took careful aim, pulling the trigger and landing a kill shot as Agent Seven pulled the trigger one last time. The bullet tore into Topher's shoulder and he bowed in pain, tripping over his own feet and landing hard on the ground, his ankle snapped audibly and he swore. Agent Seven toppled over as a horde shuffled toward the noise.

"Got him!" Topher muttered jubilantly as the door behind him gave way and the zombies descended. Topher didn't wait for the zombies to get him. He drew the handgun Aya had given him, put it in his mouth and pulled the trigger.

--

"Aya!" Connor screamed, shooting the first zombie that showed its face as he climbed through the broken window. "Aya!"

"Connor!" she replied, appearing in a doorway. She was holding an axe, dark blood dripping from the blade as she stood in the room. "There's zombies in here," she managed to croak.

"Oh, thank Christ," Connor breathed. He swivelled and shot an approaching zombie in the leg; hobbling it and making it topple to the ground. "There are zombies on the main floor, too. Come on, leave the axe, let's go." He held out a hand for Aya and she sprinted forward and grabbed it. He pulled her out of the window and back on to the fire escape. "Climb," he told her.

Aya did as she was told, Connor followed as the zombies that Aya hadn't managed to trap appeared in the window, reaching for Connor and barely missing him.

"Go go go..." Connor grunted, swinging a kick at the head of a zombie, crushing the rotting skull with the force of his kick and hurrying Aya up with a gentle shove. They collapsed onto the roof, breathing heavily.

"Holy shit, that was close," Aya breathed. "Where's everyone else?"

Connor shook his head.

"How bad?" Aya asked.

"Chloe is dead."

Aya nodded. "Where's Topher?"

"I... don't know. He was on the front step, I gave him my rifle..."

Connor scrambled across the roof to look over main street. Agent Seven's truck was empty and the horde of zombies had left his body. Topher's body was dragged out into the street where zombies were still feasting.

Connor gagged, his face turning an ashen grey as he tried not to throw up. He shuddered, and sank to the ground. "Don't look."

"That bad?"

"Topher finished the mission," Connor replied. "I think we're safe, kinda."

Aya nodded and crawled over to Connor's side. Connor wrapped his arm around her and pulled his bag closer, dropping his handgun into it. "Congrats," he muttered. "It's just us."

"We survived," Aya agreed as her bracelet began beeping, signalling the end of the game. A smile touched her lips as she leaned against Connor and closed her eyes in exhaustion.

CHAPTER TWENTY-SIX

Winner's Circle

Aya didn't react as strong hands pulled her up from her spot. She was too tired and resigned to dying to care. Connor was shouting at her but she wasn't listening, she could barely move, let alone tell Connor that it was all right. She didn't even say anything as they were loaded into the helicopter. Connor was all teeth and claws as they rummaged through his bug-out bag, taking away all the guns and ammunition, but thankfully leaving him his food and his damned rope.

Connor snatched the bag away from the officers once they were done tossing his weapons, and opened one of the bottles of water. He settled himself next to Aya and wrapped his arms around her.

"Here," Connor whispered. "Drink. You need it. We've got a ceremony to attend, haven't we?"

"How do you know that?"

"I've watched a Rapture in my time," Connor told her, sheepishly. "Don't worry about that for now though. Drink."

Aya nodded and sipped at the water, closing her eyes and leaning into Connor's shoulder as the helicopter took them the short distance to the third city the Controllers had taken over, where the headquarters had been located and where the winner's circle was waiting for them.

Aya woke up when Connor shook her, grunting her displeasure at the rude awakening. "Just five more minutes," she joked.

"Feeling better?" Connor asked.

Aya shrugged. "Do you have a plan to get us out of this one?"

"Maybe," Connor admitted, quietly. He shot a glance over his shoulder. "I can't tell you much about it, but it's all hinging on my brother having done what I asked him on the phone."

"And if he wasn't able to?"

Connor stretched his mouth in a worried gesture of uncertainty. "Well, it depends on how badly you want to off a certain person and how willing to get shot you are."

"Wounded or killed by gunshot?" Aya asked. "Because I could handle death but I'm not cut out for prison. I wouldn't last a day."

"Dunno yet," Connor replied with a smirk. "Depends a lot on things I haven't got control over."

"Then I suppose we'll make the decision when we get to that point."

Connor nodded.

"Where are we?" Aya asked, rubbing her eyes as she peered around. She didn't recognize the building.

"Heading to the winner's party, I guess?"

Aya looked herself over. She was covered in dirt, blood, sweat and soot. "Are you sure they don't want us to shower first? I mean, I'm pretty sure I've got a proper evening gown in my bug-out bag."

"That's very clever, Miss Wu. I'm sure your fans will be pleased to see that you haven't lost your sense of humour."

Connor and Aya looked over to where Hilda was standing.

"Who the hell are you?" Connor demanded.

"My name is Hilda, I am Herr Ritter's assistant. I am here to brief you and to take you to the ceremony that will officially make you two the winners of this year's Rapture."

"And what if we decline that offer?" Connor asked.

"You don't decline," Hilda warned. "Besides, there's a crowd waiting for you."

Connor looked to Aya who shrugged. "Let's just get this over with," Aya said. "Then we can worry about stuff like PTSD and therapy bills."

Connor grinned and climbed out of the helicopter. He offered Aya his hand and she took it, letting him help her out of the helicopter and onto the ground. Her legs were still shaking but she managed to stand up on her own. Connor grabbed his bag from inside the helicopter and slung it over his shoulder. He placed a hand on Aya's shoulder and stared at her for a long moment.

"You ready for this?"

Aya nodded. "Yeah, let's do it and get it over with."

Hilda waited for them, tapping her foot impatiently. Connor and Aya walked together, arms wrapped around each other's shoulder and waist for support.

"How very touching," Hilda drawled.

Connor shrugged. "Lead on, miss Hilda. The sooner we can get this hell over with, the sooner we can get to therapy."

Hilda turned on her heel and started walking. "Keep up," she snapped as armed guards fell into step, flanking Connor and Aya. "Now," Hilda explained as she walked, "you're going to be on television. Herr Ritter is announcing you two as the winners. There will be a crowd and a lot of reporters. You'll probably be asked questions. Aya, it would be in your best interest not to talk about your political bile for the time being, there will be plenty of time for you to talk about that after. Herr Ritter has not slept for three days and he is very paranoid right now," she added, looking over her shoulder. "Security is tight, and Alphonse is on the edge of snapping. I suggest that we don't make this more of a political statement than it's already become."

Aya made the motion of zipping her lips closed and throwing away the key.

"Thank you," Hilda said with a curt nod.

The procession stopped at the end of a long hallway. Aya frowned, she wasn't aware of a hangar in the town.

"We are in the town you think we are, this is a temporary hangar we've erected just for this purpose," Hilda told Aya. "It used to be a soundstage or something? We're by the river."

Aya nodded. "Thanks for clearing that up."

"Your families have been contacted, though there was mixed success in reaching them. I don't think they've arrived yet, but they do know that you're alive and well and have been announced as the winners."

Connor's jaw clenched. He hoped that his brother had managed to call in the favours he had asked for on the radio. If he hadn't... then they were stuck in the media circus, or jail, depending on how Connor's plan went. They could hear Alphonse making some sort of speech, but neither Connor nor Aya was paying attention.

"Come on," Hilda announced. "That's our cue."

Wordlessly, they followed Hilda out into the bright light. The crowd assembled went insane, cheering, shouting and the sounds of a hundred cameras all clicking all at once filled the air. Aya blinked in the bright sun and Connor scowled, scanning the crowd.

"He's here," Connor whispered, spying his brother near the stage at the far end. "There."

Aya looked where Connor indicated and saw his brother, grinning like a madman. The resemblance was striking. "All right, you got a plan?" Aya whispered.

"You still got that knife in your boot?" Connor asked.

"Yeah?"

"How much do you want Ritter dealt with?"

Aya looked up at Connor, there was no trace of humour in his face. "Do what you need, I'll follow you."

Connor nodded.

"And now," Alphonse said into the microphone, I'll turn this over to Aya and

Connor so they can say a few words, if they're feeling up to talking, that is."

Aya glared at Alphonse and he smiled, innocently, back at her. Aya stepped up to the microphone. "I didn't win," she said bluntly. "Not as long as this is still happening. I won't have won a damn thing until the Rapture is shut down for good."

The crowd cheered again, chanting Aya's name, and Alphonse darted forward to take the microphone away from her.

"You little bitch," he spat before holding his hands up to silence the crowd. "I'm well aware that you think Aya is a hero and we will be under review for the continuation of the Rapture. Believe me when I say we only care about the safety and well-being of the winners and it's a damn tragedy when the players kill each other..."

Connor stepped forward and crouched next to Aya's leg, pulling the knife from her boot as she stepped back, the rest of Alphonse's speech lost as they put their plan in motion. "On three," Connor whispered. "One... Two..."

Aya was already moving before Connor finished counting. She sprinted across the stage as Connor stood and slipped the knife up and under Alphonse's armpit. Blood poured from the wound and Connor stabbed the knife between Alphonse's ribs for good measure before following Aya across the stage. People were screaming and Hilda was shouting orders to shoot them as Alphonse Ritter coughed blood and collapsed on National Television.

No guns were fired, most of the security team had been replaced by IRA members and they moved deftly through the crowd, keeping them from stampeding, and subduing any of the security team who wasn't on their side. The crowd began chanting Aya's name as Hilda was held at gunpoint. The crowd started moving onto the stage shouting for the Rapture to be dismantled as the media tried to ensure that they got the footage they needed.

A few gunshots sounded out, bullets fired into the air and the crowd began to panic. Connor, Aya and Connor's brother rushed along the edge of the crowd to a waiting SUV. Connor and Aya climbed into the back as Connor's brother started the engine. They drove off as the rest of the IRA members dispersed the crowd and took over, shouting orders to "find Aya" and generally confusing everything even more.

"Hey," Connor's brother said, grinning into the overhead mirror.

"Christ's sakes, Mac," Connor snapped. "Couldn't have been any more subtle, could you?"

Mac grinned wider in the mirror. "Couldn't let you have all the fun."

Connor kicked the back of his brother's seat. "Aya, meet Mac."

"Hey," Mac said. "Pleasure to meet you."

"Where are we going?" Aya asked. "And my mom?"

"She knows we've got you, and she's gonna meet us. We've already transferred your winnings to a new bank account and we've got new identities set up. Connor called me and I got everything ready. Had to call in all the favours we'd saved up, Conn, but we're outta here."

"Where?" Connor asked.

"Well, we're heading to Canada."

Aya snorted a laugh and leaned back in her seat, resting her head against Connor's shoulder. Connor wrapped his arm around Aya and she fell asleep, thinking that Canada was good. They had healthcare and a no zombie policy. They'd be safe in Canada, and whatever happened to the Rapture after wasn't Aya's problem.

Acknowledgements

This book is the product of the first dream I've had in a long time, a market opening that didn't quite pan out the way I had hoped, and a teenage love of anime. This book is honestly my homage to *Battle Royale* and if you haven't read it, do so. You'll have a better understanding of why the book is paced the way it is.

I could thank everyone I've known ever, but that would take a long time, so believe me when I say thank you and assume I mean you, even if we've never met.

A profound thank you to my family however, for putting up with me writing about zombies for two years and not sleeping. I owe you.

About the Author

Kai Kiriyama lives in Canada with a stack of unread comics, and a looming deadline.

You can usually find her hanging out on Twitter, avoiding responsibility.

Kai's website:

www.theraggedyauthor.com

Kai on Twitter:

twitter.com/RaggedyAuthor

OTHER BOOKS BY KAI KIRIYAMA

Pathogen: Patient Zero

The story of a girl, her doctor, and the mystery
illness that threatens to destroy them both.

Pathogen: Outbreak

A lot can happen in 24 hours.
A patient can die.
A doctor and end up in quarantine.
And all hell can break loose.

Pathogen: Revolution

The explosive conclusion to the Pathogen series.
When you're no longer useful to society, and
survival isn't guaranteed, how far would you go
to protect those you love and guarantee your
safety?

*

Available on all digital platforms, and in
paperback.

55130146R00160

Made in the USA
Charleston, SC
21 April 2016